Mermaid KINGDOM

Secrets Beneath the Sea

by Janet Gurtler

illustrated by Katie Wood

D0047845

CAPSTONE YOUNG READERS
a capstone imprint

Mermaid Kingdom is published by
Capstone Young Readers
A Capstone Imprint
1710 Roe Crest Drive
North Mankato, Minnesota 56003
www.capstoneyoungreaders.com

Library of Congress Cataloging-in-Publication data is
available on the Library of Congress website.

ISBN: 978-1-62370-187-1 (hardback)
ISBN: 978-1-62370-681-4 (paperback)

Summary: In this compilation of three separately
published works, three mermaids in the Kingdom of
Neptunia, Shyanna, Rachel, and Cora, suffer the same
problems of growing up as teenagers everywhere.

Designer: Alison Thiele

Artistic Elements: Shutterstock

Printd and bound in the USA.
009746R

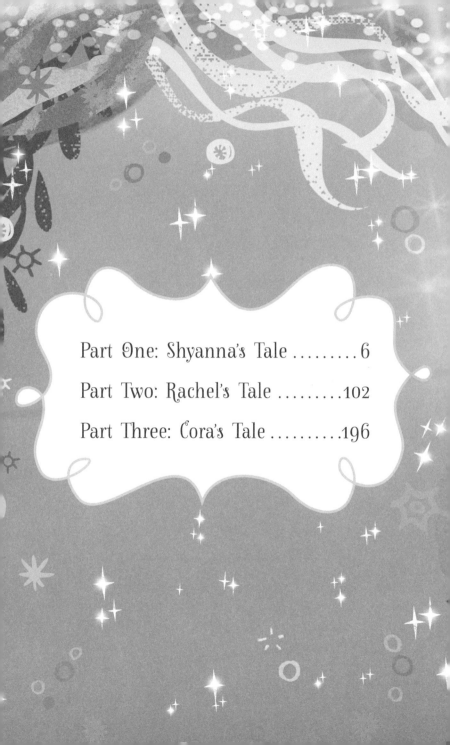

Mermaid Life

☆ Mermaid Kingdom refers to all the kingdoms in the sea, including Neptunia, Caspian, Hercules, Titania, and Nessland. Each kingdom has a king and queen who live in a castle. Merpeople live in caves.

☆ Mermaids get their legs on their thirteenth birthdays at the stroke of midnight. It's a celebration when the mermaid makes her first voyage onto land. After their thirteenth birthdays, mermaids can go on land for short periods of time but must be very careful.

☆ If a mermaid goes on land before her thirteenth birthday, she will get her legs early and never get her tail back. She will lose all memories of being a mermaid and will be human forever.

☆ Mermaids are able to stay on land with legs for no more than forty-eight hours. Any longer and they will not be able to get their tails back and will be human forever. They will lose all memories of being a mermaid.

☆ If they fall in love, merpeople and humans can marry and have babies (with special permission from the king and queen of their kingdom). Their babies are half-human and half-merperson. However, this love must be the strongest love possible in order for it to be approved by the king and queen.

☆ Half-human mermaids are able to go on land indefinitely and can change back to a mermaid anytime. However, they are not allowed to tell other humans about the mermaid world unless they have special permission from the king and queen.

Part One: Shyanna's Tale

Chapter One

I had a plan. And unlike some of my plans, this one was brilliant. I thought about it while I watched my best friend's purple tail sparkle and glitter as she swirled around Walrus Waterpark with her baby sister. Jewel was giggling with delight as Cora twirled around and around.

Cora didn't know how lucky she was. She often assured me that being a big sister was a lot of work and often annoying, but I still wanted to have a sister. Unfortunately, that wasn't really an option.

My dad disappeared two years ago. Neptunia may be the best kingdom in the ocean, but there are always dangers underwater. From humans and nets to sharks and storms, the ocean is a dangerous place to live. Anything could happen at any time, and nobody really knows what happened to my dad.

Cora glanced over. "Why do you look so sad, Shyanna?" she asked as she put Jewel down in the sandbox in the middle of the park.

"I'm not sad," I told Cora. It wasn't really a lie. Not completely. "I'm thinking." That part was definitely true. Thinking about my plan.

"Thinking?" Cora shook a finger at me. "You have that look!" Cora swam over to the swing set I was perched on and flipped around in figure eights in front of me.

"What look?" I batted my eyelashes and opened my eyes wider. Sometimes I practiced my expressions in front of a mirror, so they looked super authentic. It sounds weird, but it really does help.

"Your 'I'm about to get myself into trouble and drag Cora along in the current' look," she said. She grinned and tried to rock me off the swing. I held on tighter and laughed.

"No," I said. "I won't involve you. I promise."

"You say that every time! And every time, somehow, I'm right in the middle." Cora threw her head back and laughed. "Good thing I love you." The sound of her laugh was so enchanting that a school of curious catfish swam over to see what was happening. Cora waved them away and then swooped back to her sister, scooping her up in her arms. Jewel giggled and stared up at Cora, adoration shining in her sea-blue eyes.

"So," Cora said to me. "What is the plan?"

"I want to win the twelve-year-old age category in the Melody Pageant," I blurted out. "I mean," I corrected myself and spoke softer and slower, "I'm hoping to be selected for the finals. I know that winning isn't everything."

Everyone in the kingdom goes to the Melody Pageant. It is the biggest and oldest celebration in Neptunia. It takes place in the courtyard in Neptunia's majestic castle, where the King and Queen live. The best part of the celebration is the talent competition during the pageant. It is simply magical. And winning wasn't really my main objective, but it's always hard to rein in my competitive side.

"I entered my name yesterday!"

"You did?" Cora slid onto the bench across from me, rocking Jewel in her arms.

Every year the King and Queen select the finalists from a special conch shell. Any mermaid could enter, but I never had the nerve to try — until now. Until now, I was too scared.

But ever since my dad disappeared, my mom had been miserable. She used to swim around singing all the time. And she had the most magical voice ever! We all loved to hear her sing, especially my dad. But now she wouldn't even hum, let alone sing. I needed to bring music back to my mom. She was ready, and so was I.

Cora frowned. "You're a beautiful singer, Shy, but isn't there one problem?" she asked. "A problem with a capital *P*?"

"Stage fright," we both said at the same time.

I sighed deeply. "Maybe we could enter the duet contest. You could sing with me?" I suggested. "I'm not as nervous when I sing with other people."

Cora laughed. "I'm the worst singer in Neptunia."

"You are not!" I said.

"I prefer sports," Cora said. "But I'll do what I can to help. Like when you helped me train for the Dolphin swim meet."

Cora put the *best* in best friend. We smiled at each other, remembering the fun we'd had getting her ready for the competition. I'd worn a timer around my neck for weeks and encouraged her as she swam faster and faster. I'd cheered extra loud when a gold medal was draped around her neck.

"With your help, I can do it. I know I can," I said with confidence.

"But why?" she asked. "Why now?"

Unable to contain myself, I leaped up and swam in a circle.

"If I make it to the finals, my mom will have to come to the Melody Pageant and enjoy music again," I said.

"You really think she would go?" Cora asked.

"Yes," I replied.

"But your mom stopped singing in your cave," Cora said as she rocked her sleeping sister. Her point popped my happiness bubble.

Ever since my dad disappeared, my mom refused to go to the Melody Pageant. She wouldn't even listen to music anymore.

She believed my dad was captured in a fishing net because humans heard him singing. He'd been out in the ocean, past Neptunia, to try to find a special shell for their anniversary. He could never resist singing when he was out hunting for treasure, which was his very favorite thing to do.

"She doesn't sing because it makes her sad. But if she goes to the pageant, she'll remember that it can make her happy too! She'll see how wonderful it is!" I refused to feel guilty. It was for my mom's own good. And mine too. We needed more happiness in our cave. I wanted to be able to sing songs that reminded me of my dad.

"Did she say she wants to go?" Cora asked.

I plunked down on the bench again. "No. But I feel it. It's sort of like when she makes me eat krill medicine. I don't want to do it at the time, but it makes me feel better after."

Cora frowned.

"There is one other problem, Shyanna." Cora tapped a finger against her cheek. Her eyebrows were still pressed into a disapproving line. I already knew what she was going to say, but I still asked.

"What?" I asked.

"Your competitive spirit will take over, and you won't be happy unless you win."

I put both hands on my hips and frowned. "It won't be like that."

"Remember when you entered that sand building contest and you stayed up all night and built the biggest sand castle in the kingdom?"

"Well, I won, didn't I?" I reminded her.

"Yes, but you didn't sleep for forty-eight hours! And that time you entered the clam-eating contest?"

I bit my lip. I had refused to give up until I won, but I was sick for days afterward. Okay, so maybe I did like to win. But didn't everyone?

"Well, I have the perfect song. I just need help getting the pitch right." I frowned. "Don't you think I have a chance to win the twelve-year-old category?"

Cora reached for my hand and squeezed. "Of course you have a chance," she said. Then she pulled back. "But that's not supposed to be the point. You want to show your mom how great singing is and how happy it can make you. You want to be able to sing at home and maybe conquer your stage fright while you're at it. Right?"

"I know. This is about my mom. And remembering my dad. I promise." I closed my eyes, imagining myself singing on the stage in front of the King and Queen. I pictured a winner's crown being placed on my head.

"Shyanna?" Cora said sharply, snapping me back to reality.

I coughed and then swallowed, ignoring a tickle at the back of my throat. Instead I smiled at Cora to show her my plan wouldn't get her in any trouble at all.

"Don't worry," I said. "My plan will work. It will help my mom get her sparkle back and remind her of the positive powers of music and how much my dad loved it."

And if I happened to win my age category . . . well, how bad would that be?

Chapter Two

Boom! Bang! Bang!

Cora and I both turned when we heard the sudden noises outside of Walrus Waterpark.

"They're starting to set up!" I said.

The selection ceremony was later that day, and there was a flurry of activity. Mermen swam by, carrying colorful flags and tables. A group of mermaids followed carrying colorful sea glass jewels and huge flower decorations.

"What time does the selection ceremony begin?" Cora asked.

"At dusk." It was only a few hours away.

"Let's take Jewel home," Cora said. "We have work to do. We'll go to your cave so that I can comb out your hair and shine up your tail," Cora got up from the bench and began to swim.

I clapped my hands. Cora would make me look extra pretty.

"What seashell top are you going to wear?" she asked as I hurried along behind her. "Something green?" she said before I could answer.

"Yes! Green!" I agreed excitedly.

"The green will contrast nicely with the golden flecks in your tail. I'll rub your tail with fish oil to make it extra rainbow-like."

Like most mermaids, my tail was a mix of colors. Cora's spectacular single-shade purple tail was the envy of all of Neptunia. I'd always wanted a single-shade tail, but Cora always said she wished for a tail more like mine.

We swam past the pink coral pillars of the Queen's court tower. It was adorned with precious pearls of the sea, the official jewel for all of the mermaid kingdoms. Merpeople lit the entrance to the castle and the courtyard with jellyfish; others were hanging puffer fish lanterns in the tower above the courtyard. The majestic castle looked even more magical than normal.

It was all so exciting. I couldn't stop grinning at everyone bustling around. Everyone was happy and festive. I wanted my mom to feel some of the joy!

"Come on, Cora," I said. "We have a lot to do before the big ceremony."

"I'm coming," she said with a smile.

We swam to Cora's cave first. As the oldest sibling and the official family babysitter, Cora had to fight off the rest of her three younger sisters, all of them chattering and wanting her attention. She tucked Baby Jewel into her crib, and then Cora announced to her family that I had put my name in the conch shell. Her whole family cheered and promised to cross their fingers for me.

Her mom gave her permission to help me get ready, so Cora changed into a fancy purple shell top and off we went. She arranged to meet her family in the courtyard later to watch the selection ceremony.

Mom was still working at the Fish Factory when we got to my cave. Cora and I hurried to my room, and she got to work, helping me beautify. She combed my hair until it was free of tangles and shiny, and then she put it up in beautiful shell clips. She glossed my lips and shined my tail with special oils.

"You look beautiful, but what are you girls doing?" came a voice from my doorway. I glanced over and saw that Mom was watching us. She must have gotten home early.

"Today's the selection ceremony for the Melody Pageant," I announced, as if she didn't know and hadn't been trying to avoid it.

"I know, but . . ." she trailed off, puzzled by the primping that was going on in my room.

"I put my name in the shell," I explained.

"Oh, Shyanna," she said. She blinked, and tears filled her eyes. I was afraid she was going to cry, but then she smiled, and I realized her tears were tears of joy. "I'm very proud of you."

"You are? Really? You're not mad?" I asked.

"Of course not. You love to sing. I know that. Just like your dad. And if you're willing to take on your stage fright . . . well, that's brave and amazing."

"I really want to sing in the Melody Pageant, Mom." I held my breath as she bowed her head for a moment. I bit my lip and avoided looking at her, or I might start to cry. I didn't want to make my mom sad or upset.

"You really want a chance to sing in the pageant, Shyanna?" She took a deep breath and then let it out.

I nodded. "More than a crab loves to crawl."

"Then I hope the King draws your name," she said with pride in her voice.

"Thank you," I said. "Will you come to the selection ceremony?"

"I can't," she said. "But I promise if your name is called, I will come to the pageant. Deal?"

"Yes!" I yelled as I gave her a huge hug.

Everyone told me I got my beautiful singing voice from my mom. She told me I got her nervousness too. It was so sad that she wouldn't sing anymore. I was sure she only needed a little push to find joy in singing again. Going to the pageant would be the push she needed.

Chapter Three

The King was the most handsome merman in Neptunia, with long blond hair that flowed under his golden crown. The beautiful Queen, on the throne beside him, shimmered in the jellyfish light. The King and Queen wore dazzling purple robes made from the dye of sea snails.

The Queen looked radiant as she held up one of the conch shells filled with contestants' names. The King announced the last eleven-year-old finalist in his booming voice. The Queen put down that conch shell and picked up the conch shell with twelve-year-old names inside. This was it!

I could barely breathe as I listened to the first names being read. There were only ten spots, and they were filling up.

"Our second to last twelve-year-old is . . ."

"Rachel Marlin," the King announced.

My tail deflated. A beautiful mermaid with curly red hair swam up front. I didn't recognize her, which was weird since I knew everyone in Neptunia.

"Who's that?" I whispered, but Cora was busy with Jewel and didn't look up.

Finally the Queen held out the conch shell again.

"And the last name for the twelve-year-old competition is . . ." the King said and paused for effect. He cleared his throat.

I crossed my fingers as the seconds ticked by. Even Jewel stopped crying. Cora glanced up at the King and then at me. What was taking so long?

"Shelby Stewart."

My insides crumbled. I swallowed a lump that sprang up in my throat. I wouldn't get my chance to sing in the pageant. I wouldn't win. Worse, my mom wouldn't come to the pageant.

There was clapping, and then a pause as a mermaid with a pink and turquoise tail swam forward. She didn't swim to sit with the other finalists; instead, she swam to the Queen and whispered in her ear. The Queen nodded, gave her a hug, and then whispered something to the King.

"The last contestant is unable to compete, so I will draw again for our final competitor." The King held up a piece of paper. "The final competitor in the twelve-year-old category is . . . Shyanna Angler."

My ears roared louder than big waves crashing to shore. Cora hugged me and screamed, and I managed to swim up front. Cora and her family cheered my name extra loud.

I was in shock! I couldn't believe the King had drawn my name out of the shell! I knew it had nothing to do with skill, as it was just luck if you got chosen. But I didn't care! This was a huge moment for me!

* * *

"Mom!" I yelled when I swam back into our cave. "Mom!"

She was waiting for me in the front room. I swam into her arms, and she hugged me tight. "Cora's mom called and told me you were picked. I'm so proud of you," she said.

I let out the breath I'd been holding. "You're really not mad?"

"Of course not. It's what you wanted. You need to go after what you want. I know I've been strict about the singing," she said. "But maybe it's time to bring some joy back into our house."

"I couldn't agree more," I said with a smile. "So you're really going to come to the pageant? I don't want to sing without you there."

She hugged me again, even tighter. "Of course I'll be there," she promised. "And you must practice."

I took a deep breath. I hated to ask, but a part of me wanted to not only compete, but to win. "Do you think you could help me? I think I can deal with the stage fright, and I have my song picked, but I can't get the pitch right. Everyone says you're the best soprano singer in the kingdom."

"Oh, Shyanna," she said and swam over to the sandbag chair across the room. "I can't sing anymore. I just can't. Not since your dad . . ." She plopped down on the chair and fiddled with her tail.

I nodded and tried not to show my complete disappointment. It wasn't fair of me to even ask. She had agreed to come, and she was even encouraging me to sing again. I shouldn't push for more, even though I wanted to.

She glanced up. "I heard the Queen hired a new singing instructor. He just moved to Neptunia from Caspian. He has a daughter about your age, actually."

Caspian was the kingdom closest to the mainland. Rumor had it that some merpeople from that kingdom had met actual humans! I'd always wanted to see a human. I wondered if the singing instructor or his daughter had ever met humans.

"I'll ask if he can give you lessons," my mom said. "Your dad would have wanted that."

"Oh, thank you, Mom. Thank you!" I told her. Hearing her mention my dad again was a good sign.

"After all," she continued. "The worst he can say is no."

Chapter Four

Nothing could wipe the smile off my face as
Mom and I headed to meet the new music instructor.
Along the way, merpeople waved at me and called
out congratulations for being selected to sing at
the pageant. Being treated like a celebrity was fun!
Imagine if I actually won the pageant!

A flurry of nerves started in my stomach. I would
be singing on a stage in front of everyone, which
was really scary. But I had my mom's secret to help
fight off stage fright. I would be fine. I just had to be

confident. If I could master the song, I might even win. I just had to focus.

Cora's voice echoed in my head. "Remember. It's not about winning. You get to face your fear, and you get your mom to come to the pageant."

"Hello!" a voice called as we swam past the cave of my mom's friend, Pearl Sparkles. "So good to see you out and about!" She swam out to greet us, and the two of them started to chatter.

It was obvious my plan was already working. Mom was out of the cave and talking to her oldest friend, all because of the pageant! I twirled around in the water waiting for them to finish up, and soon I got bored. I signaled to my mom that I was going on ahead, and she nodded her permission.

I swam all the way toward the last caves at the edge of Neptunia. The voice instructor lived in a new neighborhood for the King and Queen's special helpers. Their row of caves was larger than ours, but they seemed vacant because hardly anyone lived there yet. No merpeople played in the yards or worked outside. I swam closer to the caves we were headed for, and then a sound reached me and crept into my soul.

Singing. Only it was so beautiful and haunting that I almost started to cry. The high notes melted my heart, and the low notes flowed behind them and softened my soul. The voice drifted up and down and lingered and floated, almost as if it were a living part of the water. It was the most amazing thing I'd ever heard. Even more beautiful than the most beautiful whale songs.

Mesmerized, I swam toward the sound and peered into the cave it came from. A mermaid sat on a rock, facing away from me. She had beautiful curly red hair hanging down her back. As she reached the end of the song, she turned her head. Her eyes were closed, but I recognized her profile. Oh no! It was her. The girl from the pageant. The new twelve-year-old mermaid! I swam away quickly, before she could

open her eyes and see me. I didn't want her to think I was spying on her. Her voice was so beautiful, and I knew then that I had no chance to win against her. I wanted to get away from that voice!

I hurried back through the neighborhood toward Pearl's house, but Mom met me about halfway back. "Are you okay, Shyanna?" she asked. "You look as if you've seen a ghost fish!"

"Fine," I lied. "I'm fine." I hadn't seen a ghost fish. I'd seen my pageant crown being pulled off my head. I know I kept telling myself that winning didn't matter, but it did!

Mom frowned at me but pulled me along, leading the way back to the new neighborhood. "There's the cave." She pointed at the cave where the redhead had been singing and swam on ahead toward it.

The redhead must be the instructor's daughter! No! I couldn't meet her. I couldn't. I didn't want her to know I needed help when she was already so amazing.

"Actually," I told my mom quickly, "I'm not feeling well." I treaded water and refused to follow her any farther. "And I changed my mind. I don't think I need lessons after all. I can learn the pitch myself."

She swam back to my side and smiled. "Pre-stage fright? It's okay. Don't be nervous. Come on, Shy. It's his job. He'll help you."

She took my hand and pulled me beside her until we were in front of the cave. I was so flustered that I didn't know what to do. She rang the bell, and the beautiful mermaid swam to the opening. She looked at both of us and smiled brightly. "Hello!"

"Hello! We're looking for Seth Marlin," my mom told her.

"You're Shyanna, right? From selections? It's going to be so fun! I've never sung in public before. It's all so exciting!" The girl stopped talking for a minute and turned and yelled for her dad.

She turned back to me. "I'm Rachel. His daughter." She smiled and held out her hand.

I squinted as my mom shook the hand of the girl who was going to snatch my crown from me. "Nice to meet you," my mom said. "This is Shyanna's first time singing in front of a crowd too. We heard your dad was an excellent coach. We're hoping he'll help her get her pitch just right."

I didn't say anything. I didn't want this girl to hear me sing. She'd laugh at my awful pitch. She'd know how much better she was.

"Would you like to come in and wait? I think he's on the phone talking with the Queen about her voice lessons."

"Thank you," my mom said.

"No," I said at the same time. I held my stomach. "Sick," I said. I coughed for effect. "We should go."

Rachel looked at me and moved back a tiny bit. My mom frowned. I pulled on her arm. "We should go. Now."

"Don't you want to talk to my dad first?" Rachel asked. "I'm sure he'd love to help you."

41

My cheeks were as red as lobster tails. "It's okay," I said again. "I'm not feeling well. And I'm not sure if I need a coach after all. Bye."

I swam away, not giving my mom any option but to follow. I heard her tell Rachel to apologize to her dad for us, and then she swam up beside me. I swam faster.

"Shyanna." She grabbed my tail, so I had to stop. Then she put her hand on my forehead. "You're not warm. Are you sure it isn't nerves?"

"Maybe," I said and tried to swim away.

She held my tail. "I know you're nervous, but you can't waste Mr. Marlin's time like that. It's very rude. We should go back and apologize."

"No," I cried. "I'm not going back!"

And then the sound coated the water around us — the beauty of Rachel's singing. I put my hands over my ears and shook my head, trying to keep the sound out. I knew I was acting like a baby, but I didn't care.

"Shyanna." My mom looked toward the cave and then back at me. "Is that Rachel?"

I nodded and dropped my hands from my head. "She's going to be in the pageant," I said. "And she's twelve, and she's the best singer I've ever heard in my life." I sighed.

"That doesn't matter," my mom said. "You have a beautiful voice too."

"Listen to her," I said. "She's amazing. I can't let her hear me try to reach notes I might not even be able to reach. It's embarrassing. She's obviously going to win. I shouldn't even try."

Mom crossed her arms and stuck out her lips. "Is that the reason you're suddenly feeling sick?"

I nodded and tried not to cry.

"Oh, Shyanna," she said. "You put your name in the shell and were selected. You can't back out now."

"But that —"

"Shyanna!" Mom said as she cut me off. "I'm proud of you for even trying. For facing your fears.

43

It's not always about winning. Your dad would want you to sing. He would be so proud."

She put her arm around me. "Come on," she said. "Let's go home."

She was right. I was so happy that we were talking about my dad again, and it made me happy to see her happier too. But Cora was also right. I really wanted to win the pageant. Why couldn't I make my mom happy and also be the big winner? I just had to think of a way to beat Rachel.

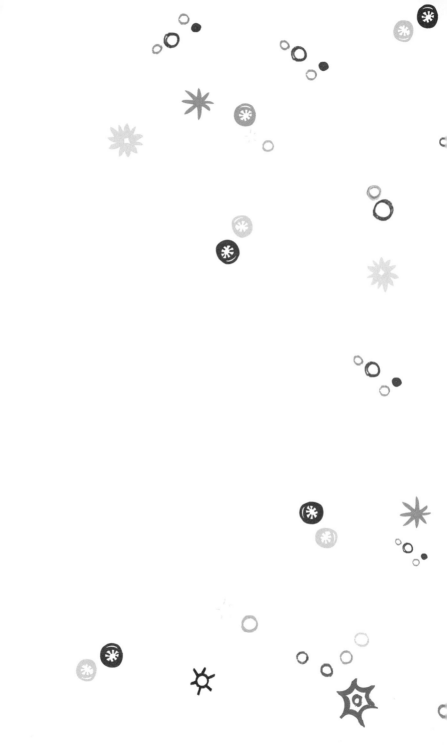

Chapter Five

The next day my throat was sore. Maybe my bad sportsmanship was actually making me sick. I gargled with sea-salt water, and that seemed to help for a while. Afterward I sang arpeggios in my room and tried the song I picked. I still couldn't get the right pitch. I needed that pitch to have any chance of beating Rachel. I thought about picking a different song, but this was my dad's favorite song. I knew it would be extra special to my mom, so there was no going back.

I sang and sang until my voice was almost gone, and then I glanced at my clock and groaned. Oh no! I was late! I was supposed to meet Cora at Walrus Waterpark ten minutes ago. I rushed out of my cave without even brushing my tangled hair.

I hurried toward Walrus Waterpark but slowed down when I got close. Cora was twirling in circles in front of the swings, which wasn't unusual since she is always moving. What made me stop and hesitate was the mermaid perched on the swing.

She had a big smile on her face, and her gorgeous hair was flowing behind her as she moved. It was Rachel. Even worse, little Jewel sat on her lap and was smiling up at her. Jewel would never swing with me. And she rarely even smiled at me. This mermaid was really starting to annoy me.

I turned around, about to swim away and go home, but Cora shouted my name. "Shyanna! You're late! Come meet Rachel. She's coming to our school next month! She'll be in our class!"

I bit my lip to stop myself from saying something mean and remembered that Cora had been distracted when Rachel's name was selected from the conch shell. Cora obviously didn't know that Rachel was my biggest competition. Plus, we didn't need another friend. We had each other.

"Great," I said. I tried to smile, but my lips wouldn't cooperate. "We've met." I floated in front of the swing set, unwilling to sit beside her. "She's singing in the pageant too," I told Cora. "In the twelve-year-old category."

"How cool! Now I have two people to cheer for," Cora said. She clearly didn't see how annoyed I was. Why was she being so nice to someone she didn't even know?

"Hi, Shyanna. Are you feeling better?" Rachel asked. She looked so genuinely concerned that I felt a little guilty about how rude I was being. In fact, I think the guilt was making me feel sick, as my throat was aching. It even hurt to swallow.

"I told my dad you stopped by," she went on. "He said he'd love to help you with your song."

"No. It's okay. I decided I don't need help." My cheeks burned. Cora was looking at me with confusion, but after hearing Rachel sing, I didn't want her dad's help. I couldn't let her know my weaknesses.

"Wah!" Jewel started to shriek, and I smiled down at her. I wanted to give her a high five, but Cora plucked her off Rachel's lap and swam in circles, trying to distract her.

"Do you want to practice together?" Rachel asked. "I love duets."

"Hey, maybe you could sing a duet with Rachel!" Cora said to me. "That would help with your —"

"NO!" I shouted before Cora could reveal to Rachel that I had stage fright.

Rachel blinked. Her smile went a little wobbly. I thought about her being new to Neptunia. She'd had to leave behind all her friends at Caspian. Then again, once everyone heard her sing, she'd have lots of new friends here. More than me, probably.

"Shyanna?" Cora said, staring at me like I'd lost my mermaid mind.

I looked away. "I mean maybe," I said. "But if you sing a duet, you can't win the category trophy."

"I thought you didn't want to win," Cora said and stopped twirling. Jewel screeched unhappily.

"I don't," I lied. "I just want to sing alone."

Cora gave me a dirty look and then tickled Jewel until she giggled.

"Swing with me?" Rachel said to me while Cora was distracted. I knew Rachel was just trying to be nice, but it was hard to be nice back. Before Rachel moved here, I was the front-runner to win the pageant. Now I barely had a chance. She was so talented and sweet it was hard to stomach it.

I reluctantly slid onto the swing beside her. I started pumping my tail hard to get up higher and higher on my swing so I wouldn't have to talk to her.

But Rachel smiled and started swinging harder too. "So," she said, "how's the school here? Are the mermaids nice?"

I bit my lip and thought about what to say. "Pretty nice." I glanced around Walrus Waterpark, avoiding her eyes. "I mean. There are lots of unspoken rules you might not know. Being new and all."

"Really? Like what?" She started swishing her tail, but lightly, so the swing only moved a little.

"Well . . ." I said and let my voice drag off.

"What?" she asked.

"Well. Since you are new here, the merkids might be kind of jealous if you win the Melody Pageant." I took one hand off the swing and tried to comb it through my messy hair.

"Really?"

"Well, I don't know for sure, but it wouldn't be great. The pageant is such a big deal."

"I know." Rachel sighed and glanced over to where Cora and Jewel were playing in the water box. "My best friend, Owen, doesn't care about the pageant," she said sadly.

"Your best friend is a boy?"

"Um . . . sort of," she said with a sad smile.

"Cool." I picked a strand of seaweed from my hair and thought about how hard it must be to leave behind your best friend.

"I don't want to win the pageant if the other merkids won't like me. Maybe I should forfeit?" she asked.

I fidgeted on the swing and cleared my throat.

"I was so nervous to enter," she said. "And now that I'm picked, I think I should go through with it."

"I only entered so my mom would have to come to the pageant. She doesn't usually go," I said.

"Really? Me too! I mean for my dad. Even though he's a singing instructor and he totally should, he hasn't been to the pageant for a few years. I was hoping to get selected so he'd have to come and see me," she said.

"Huh." I couldn't believe we actually had something in common. Our swings were moving in sync, and I glanced sideways to see her face. "Why hasn't he gone?"

Rachel stopped pumping her tail, and her swing slowed down. She lowered her eyes and looked sad. "My mom was killed by sharks a few years ago. It happened when we were traveling to the pageant. Bad memories, I guess."

I stopped pumping my tail. "I'm sorry," I said. My heart hurt for her. I could completely relate.

"Yeah. She wasn't that great of a swimmer," she says. "It was awful."

I blinked. It must have been awful. Now I felt extra bad about being so weird and mean. And I lied to her about other merkids being jealous of her. I was the only one who would be jealous.

"Hey," said Cora, who was floating toward us. "You two want to come to my house? I have to get Jewel home. She's cranky, and she needs a nap."

"Sure!" I said and jumped off the swing.

"I should get home." Rachel slid off her swing. "To help out my dad. But thanks for asking."

"You sure? We'd love if you could come." Cora narrowed her eyes at me.

"I'm sure. See you both around." Rachel waved and then darted away.

"See you soon!" Cora called after her and then turned to me, narrowing her eyes even more.

"She's competing in the Melody Pageant?" she asked as we started swimming toward her cave. Jewel hung onto her around her neck.

I nodded, trying to avoid her gaze.

"And I bet she's really good." She stopped swimming so fast I bumped into her. "I heard what you told her about the merkids not liking her if she wins the pageant. Why did you tell her that, Shy?"

My cheeks turned bright red. "Well, she'll be new. The merkids might be jealous." My voice sounded weak and unsure even to me.

"Are you sure it's not you who's jealous?" Cora asked. Jewel screeched, so Cora started swimming again. Jewel needed a nap, but it sounded like she was judging me too.

I felt my eyes tearing up. "Her voice was the most amazing voice I'd ever heard from anyone in Neptunia, and not just the twelve-year-olds."

"So?" Cora asked and stopped swimming again, patting her little sister on the back to calm her.

"I want to win." I stared down at my fins.

Cora placed her free hand on her hip. "I thought you wanted to conquer your stage fright and help your mom get singing and happiness back in her life. Why is winning so important to you?"

"Winning is important to everyone!" I said.

"If you want to win so badly, you should want to compete against the best singers," she said. "Plus, winners don't cheat and lie."

"I didn't cheat," I whispered, but I don't think she heard me.

"I'm going to go home alone," she told me. "Jewel needs a long nap."

And then she swam off, swishing her glorious purple tail behind her.

What had I done? Had I just lost my best friend over my own jealousy?

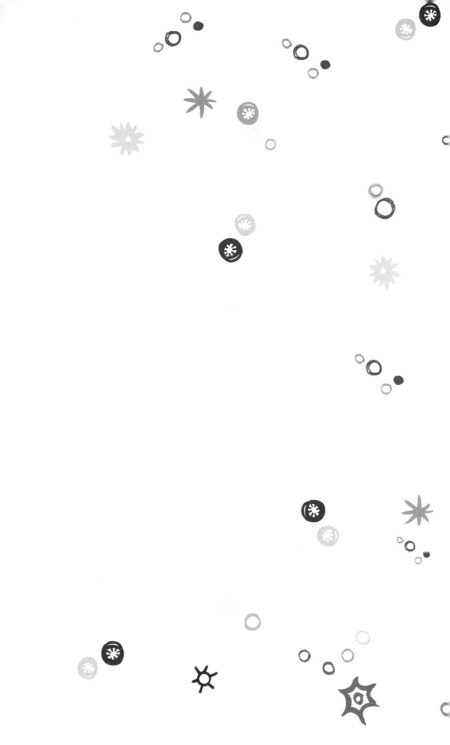

Chapter Six

My hands were shaking when I got home from the waterpark, and I was crying like a baby. Now my stomach and my throat hurt! What if Cora never wanted to talk to me again? What would I do without my best friend? I went to my room, picked up my phone, and called Cora, but there was no answer.

Cora had probably already asked Rachel to be her new best friend. Rachel was nice. And she was from Caspian. She'd probably seen humans, and she'd even had a boy for a best friend. She was much more of a merry mermaid than I was. And once everyone heard her amazing voice, she'd be the most popular mermaid at school. There wasn't much I could do about it now.

Suddenly tired, I lay down on my bed, staring at posters of my favorite bands hanging on my walls. They were gifts from Cora for my twelfth birthday. It made me start crying all over again.

* * *

"Shyanna?"

My mom's voice startled me, and I gasped. I didn't even realize I'd fallen asleep, and for a moment, I couldn't tell if it was morning or night.

"You've been sleeping?" My mom swam over and put her hand on my forehead. "You're warm," she said. "Are you feeling okay?"

The memory of everything rushed back. "I'm all right," I croaked. I didn't want to worry her. In fact, that would just make everything even worse.

"Are you nervous about the Melody Pageant?" she asked.

"No," I said quickly.

She watched me for a moment. "You're sure?"

I fake smiled and nodded.

"Come on, then. I made crab legs." I followed her to the kitchen, sat at the table, and tried to eat, but it hurt my throat to swallow.

After a while, I gave up. "I guess I'm not very hungry," I told her and pushed the plate away.

"What's wrong?" Her brow furrowed in concern.

A tear slid out of my eye. "I had a fight with Cora," I said instead of telling her about my sore throat. If I told her my throat hurt, she would pull me out of the pageant, and all this would be for nothing!

"Oh dear. What was the fight about?" She patted my head and then cleared our plates from the table.

I shrugged, not wanting to tell her what I'd done.

"I'll clean up. You get to bed. Things will look better in the morning. You and Cora will make up."

She swam over and hugged me tight and then shooed me off to bed.

I went back to my room, but before I lay down, I picked up my phone to call Cora one more time. She didn't pick up. With a heavy heart I tucked myself under the covers on my bed, and exhausted, fell fast asleep. All night long, I dreamed about being trapped by humans and living all alone in a giant fish bowl.

* * *

When I woke up in the morning, my head was pounding. Swallowing hurt. Breathing hurt. This was not good.

"Hello?" I said to my pet snail, Speedy, to try out my voice. It worked but sounded a little off. After going to the kitchen to gargle with seawater, I tried to sing. Ultra relieved to hear my singing voice work, I opened wider to hit a high note.

That's when it happened. A horrible crack. It sounded like a seal barking.

I tried again. Worse.

Sighing, I wrinkled up my nose, got out the dreaded krill medicine from the top cupboard, and swallowed back a whole tablespoon. I attempted the high note again.

Seal bark. This was serious.

Panicking, I hurried to the bookshelf and took out the *Magic Mermaid's Book of Cures* that all mermaids received when a merbaby was born. The *Magic Mermaid's Book of Cures* is only to be used in emergencies. Mermaid magic is not something the King and Queen encourage us to fool around with. They limit the use of magic, because their job is to keep merpeople safe. All merpeople know that magic has risks and shouldn't be used for fun.

I flipped to the symptom page and pinpointed the problem. Laryngitis. There was a cure, but the picture and description made my heart skip a few beats. A crushed red dwarf mussel shell would cure the throat infection, but they were only found on

Platypus Island. The island was outside of Caspian, which was close to land. Merkids couldn't leave Neptunia alone until they turned thirteen, and I was only twelve. And even when we turn thirteen, it's not safe to go so close to land.

I tried calling Cora one last time, not sure if I wanted her to come with me or talk me out of it, but she didn't pick up. That settled it. I had to go on my own. Laryngitis couldn't stop me from getting my mom to the Melody Pageant. I needed that cure. It might be dangerous, and not very smart, but what other choice did I have?

Chapter Seven

No one even paid attention as I swam past the gates that marked the entrance to Neptunia. With the Melody Pageant coming up, merpeople were too busy to notice me. I swam on and on past kingdoms I'd only visited briefly with my parents.

It was lonely and kind of scary until a whale and a group of dolphins swam up beside me. It's hard to be afraid or sad when swimming with a whale and dolphins. We all swam farther and farther until we finally reached Caspian. It was as beautiful as I'd

heard and almost as big as Neptunia. On the far side of Caspian were the gates to enter Platypus Island, and a big problem for me.

Sharp-eyed Octopi guarded the gates, but I had an idea. Distraction.

I told my dolphin friends the plan, and they whistled and clicked their approval. The whale watched from his side eye and frowned. I patted his belly, letting him know I'd be all right.

"I have to get a special shell," I told him, "to cure my voice."

The dolphins darted ahead. My whale friend couldn't come any farther because the passage narrowed, and his oversized body wouldn't fit through.

Then the dolphins got to work. They jumped and swirled and dragged their bellies on the bottom of the sea, whipping up an instant underwater sandstorm. It gave me enough time and camouflage to swim past the guards.

71

It was instantly darker once I entered Platypus Island, and fear bubbled under my fins. I glanced around nervously and tried to remember where the red dwarf mussel shells were located. I'd memorized the map that was in the *Magic Mermaid's Book of Cures*. I just had to stay calm and focus.

I swam and swam but couldn't find the shells. Then I noticed that the tide was beginning to go out. I had to find the shells and get home. I swam close to the shore and began to search. I looked and looked. The water was getting shallower. It frightened me, but I couldn't leave until I found the shells.

Suddenly, a red shimmer caught my eye. It was a red dwarf mussel shell! I dove deep, but a wave lapped over me, and the shell disappeared under the sand. Sighing, I forced myself to slow down so I would not disturb the water, and soon I saw it again — another flash of red!

I dove down fast, and my fingers grabbed at it. The sand drifted around, but I held on. The shell was mine! I had the cure! I'd be able to sing in the Melody Pageant. If I could convince Rachel not to sing, I might even win! I kicked my tail hard to swim away, but a piercing pain stopped me.

"Ouch!" I yelled. My fin was wedged underneath a rock. I wiggled around, trying to pull my tail out without dropping the shell. But the movement just made it worse. The pain was terrible!

The water continued to recede with the tide, and then my tail was only covered in a thin layer of the salt water my gills needed to keep my tail intact. The tide was going out quickly, and with each wave, less and less of the shore was undcrwater. I was going to get stuck on land if the water kept receding. This was not good. Not good at all.

If I got stuck on land now, I'd get human legs early, and my mermaid tail would never grow back. I would be stuck on land forever! I would never be able to return to Neptunia, and I wouldn't be able to call myself a mermaid ever again! And as soon as my tail was gone, my mermaid memories would be gone as well. I wouldn't remember ever being a mermaid.

My mermaid life would totally disappear.

My panic increased as the water got lower and lower. Pulling didn't help, and I started crying. I didn't want to be alone, stuck on land forever, never able to get my tail back. I wanted to stay a mermaid.

The water lapped out farther. My crying got louder and louder.

"Hello?" called a sweet voice from the shoreline above the rocks. "Are you all right down there?"

I clapped my free hand over my mouth. It was a human! Was I going to end up like my dad — lost and never to return undersea again?

Chapter Eight

"I'm coming down to help," the voice called. It was definitely a human voice.

Oh no! I couldn't let myself be seen by a human! Humans and merpeople do not mix. If I talked to a human before my thirteenth birthday, I would lose my tail forever. I would have legs for the rest of my life!

All of these rules about humans and merpeople interacting were to protect Mermaid Kingdom and all the merpeople. Only in special circumstances were merpeople and humans allowed to mix (and only with the magic protection of the King and Queen), and even I didn't fully understand what those circumstances were. All I knew was that if a human saw me, I would lose my tail and be stuck on land forever with no mermaid memories.

I was pretty much out of options. Either I was stuck on land and would get my legs too early (forgetting my entire mermaid life and becoming a human forever), or a human would talk to me and I would get my legs too early (forgetting my entire mermaid life and becoming a human forever).

The human jumped down to the rocks. She was getting closer and closer. I closed my eyes, as if it that would make anything better. Maybe if I couldn't see the human, she wouldn't bother me? I just didn't know what else to do.

"Shyanna?" the human called. "Are you stuck?"

How did this human know my name? I wondered. I opened my eyes. It was Rachel!

Rachel was a human?

"Rachel?" I gasped. "But your tail . . . you have legs." I started crying as she bent down and pulled at the rocks to release my tail. "What are you doing? You're only twelve. You'll never get your tail back!"

Had I done this to her? Made her go to shore too early? Was it all my fault? I didn't like her very much, but that didn't mean I wanted to ruin her entire life!

She ignored me and focused on freeing my tail. She pulled so hard it hurt more than sea urchin stings, but I was free!

"Swim, Shyanna, swim," she said. "You need to swim now."

I was too shocked to move. Rachel had rescued me, but she'd never be a mermaid again. Then Rachel dove into the water, and a fin flapped, splashing my face. Her tail had reappeared. I stared at it and then up at her face.

She swam on, tugging me behind her, pulling so hard that the shell I was holding fell out of my hand. I screamed, but Rachel dove deep and came up holding out her hand. The red dwarf mussel shell was inside.

She put the shell in my hand. "I hope it was worth all this trouble." Rachel swam slowly, but I grabbed her with my free hand.

"Did you lie about your age?" I asked. "Are you already thirteen?"

"I'm twelve." Rachel rolled her eyes in annoyance. "What were you doing so close to land? You could have been seen by humans."

"But you had . . . legs . . ." was all I could manage. "Your tail . . ."

Rachel sighed and rolled her eyes again, but at least she started talking. "My mom was human before she became a mermaid, which is why she couldn't swim as fast as the other mermaids. My dad fell in love with her when he spent time on shore. Because their love was so strong, she was given special permission from the Queen to become a mermaid and marry him. That makes me half-human. I can go on land whenever I want. For as long as I want."

"You can?" My mouth wouldn't close. "That is . . . so . . ." I tried to think of the word.

"Freakish?" she said and glared at me.

"Cool," I told her. "That is so cool."

She tilted her head. "Really? You don't think I'm a freak?"

"How could I think you are a freak? I think you're amazing," I said. "You saved my life!"

"What were you doing alone outside Neptunia, anyway?" she asked.

I glanced at the shell in my hand. "Something is wrong with my throat. I can't sing very well, and I needed a cure." And then something occurred to me. "Wait a minute. What were *you* doing outside Neptunia all alone?"

"I was visiting Owen. I heard you crying as I was leaving. And lucky for you I did!"

"You were with your best friend from Caspian?" I asked.

"Owen is a human," she said casually, and then she somersaulted.

Human? Rachel was so glamorous. Wait until Cora found out! But then I remembered. Cora wasn't talking to me.

"Rachel?" I called. Her eyes were wide, her mouth wider. She looked frozen. A shiver ran down my tail. I turned my head.

Sharks! And they were heading right for us.

Chapter Nine

The sharks advanced slowly as though they were taunting us. They grinned to show off rows of pointed teeth. My heart pounded. My eyes almost bulged out of my head. I fumbled and reached for Rachel's arm. "Swim. Come on, Rachel! Swim!"

She didn't move. "Shortfin Mako," she whispered without blinking. "The fastest shark in the ocean. They killed my mom." The sharks kept moving closer, not even bothering to chase us yet.

Rachel started to cry.

"No!" I said. We wouldn't go down like this. Eaten by sharks. I needed to sing in the Melody Pageant to make my mom happy again. Plus, I really didn't want to die yet.

Then I remembered the bedtime story my mom read to me over and over when I was small. The story was about mermaids with voices so powerful they could stun sharks into submission. I glanced down at my dwarf shell, crushed it in my hand, and tossed it in my mouth. Then I began to hum the song I was planning to sing in the pageant.

"Sing," I told Rachel, but she was so terrified she didn't move or take her eyes off the sharks.

"Mermaid music, hear us now," I sang. The sharks didn't stop. I cleared my throat as the last of the crushed shells dissolved.

"Mermaid magic, show us how." My voice rang clearer. My pitch was perfect!

The sharks stopped. Rachel glanced at me. I nodded, encouraging her to join me. She had to know the song. It was a mermaid classic. The sharks started moving toward us again. I sang louder.

"Mermaids sing together and free."

Rachel smiled. The song finally seemed to break her from her spell. She reached for my hand and sang the next chorus with me.

"The music we make rules the sea." Our two voices blended together, powerful and perfect. We lifted our chins and belted out the next verse.

The sharks stopped, and their eyes glazed over and rolled back. They looked like they'd gone to sleep. "It's working," I whispered. "Keep singing."

We sang another verse, and the sharks didn't move. "Go, go, go!" I whispered. Rachel and I kept holding hands, and I swam faster than I had ever swum before. Cora would have been proud. We raced back into Neptunia and into safety.

Once we were inside the kingdom, I finally stopped, bending over. I was out of breath but completely exhilarated.

Rachel threw her arms around me, and we hugged and laughed with relief.

"Thank you," Rachel said. "You saved my life. I was so scared. I couldn't think or move."

"I guess we're even now," I told her.

She stopped smiling. "Even," she agreed. And then she took a deep breath. "But I need to ask you for a favor."

I nodded. After that near-death experience, I felt almost as close to her as I did to Cora.

"Anything," I told her. "What favor?"

She bit her lip and glanced around, but the sea creatures around us weren't paying us any attention.

"Don't tell anyone," she whispered, refusing to look at me. "Please."

"You mean about . . ." I pointed down to her tail.

She finally looked at me, still biting her lip and looking nervous.

"Sure, if that's what you want. But why? It's so cool!" I said.

"Some merpeople don't understand. Everyone at Caspian knew, and I didn't have friends. I used to go to shore a lot. That's how I met Owen."

It was obvious that the other mermaids were just jealous of her, which was exactly how I had felt as well. Rachel was fabulous. And she could use legs whenever she wanted! I felt so bad for the way I had acted toward her.

"That won't happen here," I told her. "I'll make sure of it." I rushed forward and hugged her tight, ashamed of myself for being mean to her before.

"Everyone is going to love you. Especially when you win the Melody Pageant."

Her face brightened, but she shook her head. "I thought you said it was a bad idea to enter."

"No," I admitted. "The truth is, if you sing, you'll win for sure, and everyone from school will be excited. They'll want to be your friend!"

"You really think so? That's not what you said before," Rachel said.

"I know, and I'm sorry. I was really jealous of you," I said.

Before Rachel could answer, we heard someone yelling for us.

"Oh my goodness, there you two are," a voice called loudly.

We both looked ahead. Cora swam toward us. "I've been looking everywhere for you two. Your parents are worried. They're out together now, searching the other kingdoms. What have you been up to?"

Rachel and I exchanged a look. I nodded. I'd keep the secret for now. "Are you still mad at me?" I asked Cora instead of answering her question.

Cora crossed her arms and narrowed her eyes.

"I told Rachel the truth," I said quickly. "That if she sings in the pageant, all the girls will fight to be her friend."

"Then I'm not mad anymore. Not at all." Cora rushed forward and hugged us both. "I was really worried about both of you. Thank goodness you're both safe!"

"Let's get back," Cora said. "You have to get ready to sing in the pageant."

That's right, I thought. *All of this, and I still have to perform in public.* It made me more nervous than I had been when I left Neptunia alone.

Chapter Ten

The morning of the Melody Pageant, my mom helped comb my hair until it was as smooth as polished sea glass. She placed the flower and shell headpiece Cora had made on my head. My mom had even bought me a new top. It sparkled and shined and made me feel like a princess.

Once my mom finished helping me get ready, Cora and I swam over to Rachel's cave to do our final primping together. It was so fun! Every once in a while, Rachel's dad popped in and out of her room to make sure we were all doing okay. He was such a good dad.

"Do you want help with your song?" he asked. "You never did ask me to coach you."

"I'm okay," I told him. "But thank you." The mussel shell seemed to have solved my voice problems. My notes were strong, and my pitch was even. All I needed to do was conquer my nerves.

Just then my mom showed up. Mr. Marlin and my mom had agreed to get to the pageant early to save us good seats. It was such a relief to see my mom excited about singing again and going out with a new friend. On top of that, she was smiling!

"We'll take you girls out for a celebration after the show, no matter who wins," Mr. Marlin said.

"Rachel's going to win," I said.

"Shyanna's going to win," Rachel said at the same time.

We looked at each other and giggled.

"It doesn't matter who wins," my mom said.

"Just go out there, and sing your hearts out! And don't forget to have fun."

It warmed my heart to hear her say that. Maybe someday she'd start singing again too!

Finally, when it was time to go, Cora, Rachel, and I swam side by side toward the courtyard. My heart felt like it was going to burst open like a frost flower on ice. The day would be filled with music, food, friends, and happiness.

We swam into the courtyard. It looked even more amazing than it had the day of the selections. The stage was lit up with glowing jellyfish. Sea flowers in full bloom lined the seats in the audience. Everything was bright and colorful. Shells and jewels sparkled on the thrones of the King and Queen.

Suddenly, a curtain came down in front of the stage, and the jellyfish dimmed their lights. The curtains flew open, and the pageant began with a beautiful group song from last year's winners. The water vibrated with the sound, and then the pageant was underway. I clapped and mouthed along with contestants, and then before I knew it, the King was calling the twelve-year-old finalists to the stage.

I was so nervous I couldn't get up. I didn't move until Rachel grabbed my hand and pulled me with her to the seats on the side of the stage where contestants waited for their turn to perform. It felt like I was dreaming. This didn't feel real at all.

But just a few minutes later, the King announced my name. "Next up is Shyanna Angler! Let's hear it for Shyanna!"

The piano player began playing my song. I stared out at the audience. Rachel elbowed me in the side. I didn't move. The pianist paused and then replayed the introduction to my song. I didn't move.

"Shyanna," Rachel whispered. "It's your turn. Go! Sing for your mom!"

Some people in the audience started to mumble. The King and Queen stared at me. My face burned. I was too terrified to move.

I closed my eyes and tried to remember what my mom had told me. She'd told me to imagine that all of the mermaids were her. It should have helped. It should have relaxed me.

But it didn't. I couldn't move.

And then fingers gently brushed my shoulder. I opened my eyes. Cora floated in front of me, holding out her hand. "Come on," she whispered. "I'll sing it with you. You can do this, Shyanna."

I shook my head. Cora kept tugging, and Rachel looked back and forth at us. She floated up from her seat, gave Cora the thumbs-up signal, and then swam to my other side. They each took one of my hands.

"Shyanna Angler and I have decided to perform as a group instead of solo," Rachel announced to the audience. "Along with our friend, Cora Bass."

"No," I hissed to Rachel. "If you sing with me, you'll forfeit your chance to win our category."

We'd both be disqualified from the twelve-year-old category.

"Never mind," Rachel said through her teeth, smiling. She gestured toward the confused-looking pianist. The Queen clapped her hands and nodded her approval. The pianist started the song from the beginning one more time.

Rachel began to sing. She sounded amazing. Cora opened her mouth and sang along in a lower range. She smiled the special smile of a true best friend, and with the two of them encouraging me, I was pulled out of my stupor. And then, as if we'd rehearsed it a million times, we sang and harmonized the rest of the song. It sounded incredible!

When we finished, the entire crowd went crazy. Merpeople clapped their hands and floated up into a standing ovation. It was amazing! Even the King and Queen looked impressed.

I gazed into the audience, my heart filled with happiness and love, and spotted my mom. She was smiling, bursting with pride. Her face glowed. She looked happier than I could have hoped.

Finally the King waved his hands to quiet the audience. "A spectacular performance," he announced, "but not eligible for the twelve-year-old category."

I looked at Rachel to see if she was disappointed, but she smiled.

"That was the best! It doesn't matter that we can't win," she said.

"It really doesn't," I agreed. And surprisingly, that was the truth. I knew we'd be best friends for life, and that was the biggest win of all.

The King called for the next contestant, and as we swam back to our seats, Cora swam in close. "I knew somehow you'd drag me into your plan," she whispered to me and laughed.

It was the best Melody Pageant I'd ever been to, and maybe, just maybe, the best day of my life so far. There would be singing in our cave from now on!

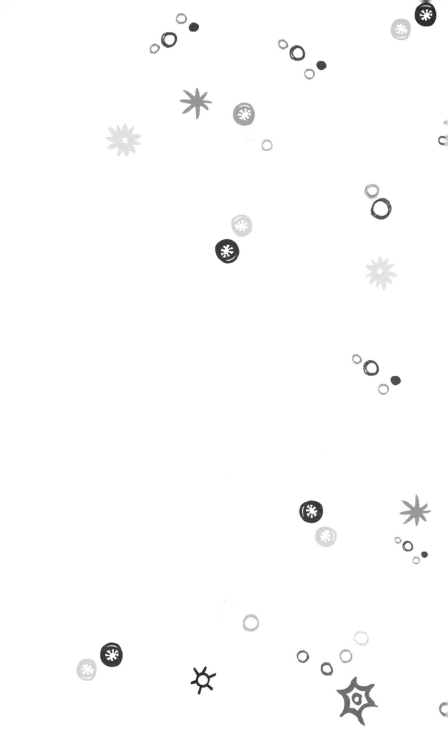

Part Two: Rachel's Tale

Chapter Eleven

Shyanna and Cora were chasing each other around, laughing so hard that tears were falling down their rosy cheeks.

"Come on, Rachel!" Shyanna shouted to me.

My friends flipped in circles, swishing their glorious sparkling mermaid tails behind them. I smiled from the swing where I sat watching them, loving my two new friends with all my heart.

"Remember when, at your twelfth birthday party, you tried to convince Alexa you were thirteen?" Cora asked Shyanna. She looked at me and explained, "Alexa almost went to shore to see Shyanna's legs."

"Oh, I still feel terrible about that," Shyanna said.

"Only because you got in so much trouble!" Cora added.

They both giggled, and I had to admit that a teeny part of me felt left out. I was new to Neptunia. After my mom died, our entire life changed. My dad and I needed a new start, and moving to Neptunia was just what we needed. We'd just moved here.

I was lucky to have two best friends already, but it didn't make everything perfect. I missed my old best friend, Owen, every day. Sometimes I even missed living in Caspian and being closer to land. It was easier to go to shore and meet up with Owen from there.

Yep, Owen was a human. And having a human as a best friend had its challenges, especially since he didn't know that I'm a mermaid. Confused yet? Here's the deal: My mom was human before she became a mermaid. My dad fell in love with her when he spent time on shore. Because their love was so strong, she was given special permission from the King and Queen to become a mermaid and marry him. I was half-human. I could go on land whenever I wanted for as long as I wanted. It really was an incredible love story.

Shyanna was the only one who knew my big secret, and I intended to keep it that way. It was hard enough being the new mermaid in Neptunia. I couldn't even imagine how freaked out the other mermaids would be if they knew I was half-human!

"I can't wait for my real thirteenth birthday," Shyanna said as she twirled around. "I can't wait to get my legs! My leg ceremony is going to be so great!" Her eyes opened wider, and she glanced at me. "I mean, the ceremony is only part of it. Having legs and visiting land will be the best part."

I knew she was trying to make me feel better. I wouldn't have a legs ceremony on my thirteenth birthday. Since I was half-human, I already had my legs. I could go on land whenever I wanted for as long as I wanted. No matter what, I'd always be a little bit different. I knew it was okay to be different, but that didn't make it easy.

I didn't even bother to tell Cora and Shyanna that my thirteenth birthday was the next day. It wasn't the big deal it would have been if I were a real mermaid, so I didn't want them to know.

Cora swam over to the swings and floated around me. "Hey, you! There's no need to look unhappy when you could be playing tag with us!" Cora squealed. She grabbed my arm and playfully pulled me off the swing. "Come on, I need your help! Shyanna gets a little crazy when we play tag."

I couldn't help laughing and dashed after Shyanna with her. It was hard to stay miserable for long with my two new friends. I raced after Shyanna, but Cora ended up catching her first. Cora was the fastest swimmer I'd ever seen!

We were still laughing when a royal trumpeter and messenger swam into Walrus Waterpark. We immediately stopped and floated at attention. The trumpet player lifted his trumpet to play the royal fanfare. A purple royal flag dangled from the middle of the trumpet as he blew out the royal tune.

When he finished, the messenger unrolled a scroll, cleared her throat, and began to read. "The Queen would like to invite Rachel Marlin, Cora Bass, and Shyanna Angler to appear with her in a Royal Concert," she announced. "Queen Kenna has requested you sing as her opening act a week from today in the Royal Gardens."

"Of course!" we all squealed in delight. That was an incredible honor! Our showstopping performance at the Melody Pageant had clearly not gone unnoticed by the Queen.

One of the reasons my dad and I had just moved to Neptunia was so he could be the Queen's singing instructor. That's how I met Shyanna and Cora. It's a long story, but I basically saved Shyanna, then she saved me, and then all three of us ended up singing together and becoming best friends. I guess the story wasn't that long.

"Wow!" Cora said. "I never thought I'd be invited to sing with the Queen!"

"It must be because of the Melody Pageant," I said. "She told my dad how impressed she'd been with us!"

Shyanna and Cora swam in little circles and shrieked with excitement again. Their energy was definitely contagious.

"My dad hinted that she might have a concert," I confided to them. "She's improved so much, and I think she wants to show off a little."

I hated to brag, but my dad really was the best singing coach in all the Mermaid Kingdoms.

"I have to get home to tell my sisters," Cora said. "They'll be thrilled — and jealous!"

"I need to tell my mom!" Shyanna said.

My dad already knew, and the only other person I wanted to tell was Owen. But I couldn't do that, of course. He didn't even know I was a mermaid. I wished so much that I could share my secret with him, but that wasn't possible, no matter how hard I wished.

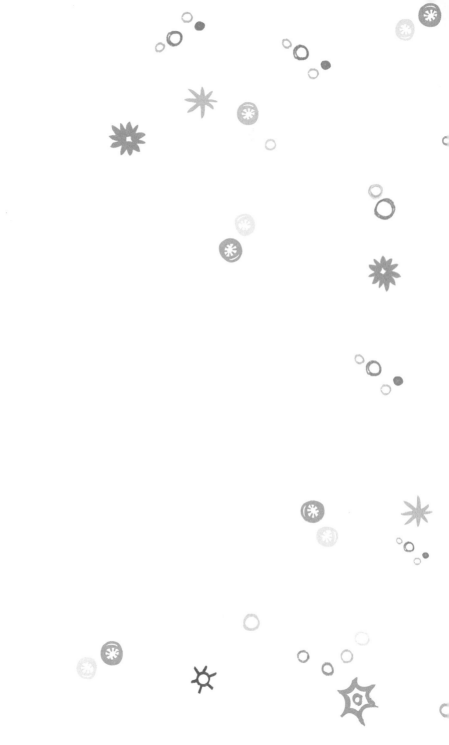

Chapter Twelve

When I woke up the next day, my dad was already at work. I was a little disappointed that he was gone. It was my birthday, and I was all alone. However, he did leave me a nice note telling me to get ready for our fun day together. He was going to be home after lunch.

Dad and I had planned a father-daughter day. We were going to spend our time exploring out in the ocean. He'd been so busy since we'd moved to Neptunia. The Queen and her royal mermaids were all taking voice lessons, which took up a lot of time. We'd hardly had any time together.

I spent the morning braiding and beading my hair and polishing up my tail. I was so excited for our day together that I was waiting at the door for him to come home. But as soon as he swam inside, I could tell our plans were not going to work out.

He pulled a bouquet of flowers out from behind his back. "Happy birthday, Rachel. I hate to do this, but our plans have to change. I'll be home a little late, but we'll celebrate then. I promise I'll make it up to you." He could tell I was disappointed.

"That's fine," I said, but I didn't mean it.

"I'm really sorry, honey," he said. "The Queen requested an extra rehearsal this afternoon, and I couldn't get out of it."

"Thanks, Dad," I said. I was trying really hard not to cry.

"I wish we had planned you a party. You are thirteen, after all," he said, frowning.

"No," I told him. "I didn't want to make a fuss about it."

He kissed my forehead. "You're so much like your mother. She never wanted to have parties for herself either. Could you at least go see Shyanna and Cora? I'll be home with cake later. I'm so sorry."

"It's okay," I told him. "It's not your fault. You work for the Queen. We knew you'd be busy!"

He rushed back to work, and I called Shyanna. Her mom said she and Cora were at the waterpark with Cora's sister, so I swam over there. When I arrived, I saw them pushing Cora's littlest sister on the swings.

"Wow!" Shyanna said when she spotted me. "You look amazing! What's the occasion?"

"Not much," I said. "I was supposed to go out with my dad, but he's busy with the Queen for the rest of the day."

"Aww," Shyanna said. "That's too bad. I bet you were really looking forward to it."

She swam over to touch my hair. "How did you do that to your hair? It's so pretty."

"It looks incredible!" Cora agreed, and she swam over to check out my red braids.

"Cora, you should wear yours like that for your thirteenth birthday!" Shyanna said.

"Great idea." The girls fussed over my hair and admired the sparkles and glitter I'd added to my tail. But soon baby Jewel started to cry, so my friends swam back to the swings and started pushing again.

"I can't wait for my leg ceremony!" Cora said. "Mostly so I can go on land and get some peace and quiet for a few hours."

I smiled at her. Her life was so different from mine. She was always busy babysitting her sisters or helping her mom around the house. She rarely had time alone, which was something I had plenty of!

"I can't wait to have cake!" Shyanna shouted. "With oyster frosting!"

Cora laughed. "You always want to have cake."

"Yes. Like today is Friday. There should be cake!" Shyanna joked.

I smiled, but then it clicked. Friday!

When I lived in Caspian, Friday was the day I'd always gone to visit Owen. Now I realized I had the perfect opportunity. Who better to see on my birthday now that dad was busy with the Queen? It took longer to swim to shore to see Owen now that I lived in Neptunia, but I had extra time.

"Um . . . I have to get going," I said and somersaulted in delight.

"Where are you going?" Cora asked.

"Just back to my cave to relax," I said. I hated to lie to Cora, but I couldn't tell her the truth.

Shyanna and I exchanged a knowing look. I waved and smiled at them as I swam as fast as I could out of the waterpark. The sooner I could get to Owen, the better!

Chapter Thirteen

I stumbled on the rocks and raced up the beach. My legs always felt a little wobbly and unsteady when they first changed over from my tail. I coughed, getting used to breathing in fresh air instead of filtering ocean water through my gills.

I was at the spot where I'd first met Owen. This was also the same place where Shyanna almost got her legs too early when she went searching for throat medication. This was the spot where I saved her and our friendship was established. This was truly one of the best spots in the world. So many incredible memories were made here.

"Hey, clumsy!" a voice yelled.

"Owen!" I jumped up and down, waving. I ran toward him, and even though I'm not a great runner, managed to get to his side quickly. I stopped, suddenly a little shy. "It's so good to see you."

"I had a feeling you were finally going to show up!" Owen said. "It's Friday! You always used to show up on Fridays." He stared at me for a second. "You look really nice."

"Thanks," I told him. "And sorry I haven't been here in a while. I've had trouble getting away."

Since my mom had died and we moved to Neptunia, it was a lot harder to see Owen. He didn't know why I couldn't see him as much, but he never questioned it. He was a good friend.

"Well, I'm glad you're back," he said. "Especially since it's your birthday!" He grinned and then started walking, gesturing for me to follow.

"You remembered?" I couldn't wipe the grin from my face as I scrambled to follow him.

"Of course I remembered!" he said, turning to me with his familiar sparkling grin. "Come on!"

"Where are we going?" I asked.

"My house," he said. "I had a feeling you'd show up, and I asked my mom to bake you a cake. Just in case. Don't tell the guys, but I think you're secretly her favorite friend of mine."

"She baked me a cake?" That made me so happy I almost cried. As we walked, I made a promise to myself to see Owen every Friday from now on. No more excuses.

"My mom loves you, and she loves baking cakes," Owen told me. "It was a win-win for her."

"She is the best!" I said.

"Justin, Mitchel, and Morgan are on their way over," Owen says. "They're at swim practice, but when they heard my mom made cake, they couldn't be stopped!"

His other friends were always nice to me too. It made me wonder why some mermaids are afraid of humans.

When we got to his house, his mom said, "Rachel! You're here!" Then she went into the kitchen and brought out the cake she had made.

She'd decorated the cake like a beautiful redheaded mermaid. My eyes bulged out of my head.

She laughed. "Don't you like it? I'm sorry. I only raised boys. I assumed all girls loved mermaids as much as I do! I've always wished they were real."

"Me too," I told her with a big grin. "I love it!"

The three boys barged in the front door then, just in time for cake.

Owen's mom put candles on the cake, lit them with a match, and they all sang "Happy Birthday" to me. We each stuffed ourselves with cake, and then Owen stood up and left the kitchen. He came back holding a pretty pink gift bag and put it on the table in front of me.

"A present? Is Rachel your girlfriend?" Morgan teased, grinning.

Owen's face turned red, and I felt my face get hot. I avoided looking at him when I reached inside the bag. I took out a box. Inside was a beautiful shell necklace.

"Do you like it?" Owen asked. "I can exchange it if you don't. Mom helped me pick it out."

"It's perfect!" I told him and immediately put it on. I decided I might never take it off.

His friends made embarrassing whistles and kissy noises.

"We're just friends," Owen said. He looked extra cute when he blushed. Not cute in a boyfriend way, either. He will always just be my best friend, which was all I wanted.

I wished I could stay longer, but I knew I should get back to Neptunia. I reluctantly thanked Owen's mom for the cake. "I have to get going. My dad will expect me home soon," I said.

"I'll walk you back to the beach," Owen offered.

He thought I lived in a house close by, and he never went farther than the edge of the beach with me. I had made it seem like my dad was super strict, because that seemed like the best excuse. I'd wait an extra five minutes to make sure Owen was gone, and then I'd slip back in the water and return to life in the sea. Thankfully Owen wasn't very snoopy, or things would fall apart fast.

"I wish you were around more," Owen said when we reached the edge of the beach. His cheeks were a little red again. "How come you aren't coming by as much as you used to?"

I stared at my feet. "I wish I could tell you," I whispered. "But you wouldn't understand."

I couldn't tell Owen I was a mermaid — or even half a mermaid. The secret was protected by mermaid magic. If I told him without special permission from the Queen or King, I'd never get my tail back and I'd have to live as a human forever.

After a few months without my tail, I'd forget that I'd ever been a mermaid at all. I knew the rules.

"Is everything okay?" Owen asked.

"Everything is great! I promise," I told him. "I have a couple of new mer . . . friends. And they're great. I'm busy. But I miss you too." Owen knew I'd had a rough year, but he didn't know I'd moved to a new Mermaid Kingdom. Obviously.

"You're sure?" he asked.

"Everything is great, I promise," I said.

"Okay," he said. "But remember . . . there's nothing you could tell me that would make me not want to be your friend."

I smiled. "Thanks, Owen," I said.

"Will you be back next Friday?" he asked. "I'm having a party at my house."

"It's your thirteenth birthday," I said, suddenly remembering.

But then I remembered that Friday was the concert too.

He looked at my face. "What's wrong?"

I dropped my gaze to my toes. "I can't believe it," I said. "I'm in a concert that night. Singing for the Queen — uh, I mean, someone really important. I'm committed to it. I'm so sorry." Telling Owen I couldn't be at his party felt worse than stepping on a stingray.

Owen ducked his head down. "No. It's okay," he said, but he couldn't hide his disappointment.

There was no way to back out of singing, but there was also no way I could miss Owen's birthday party. Especially when he went out of his way to make mine so great!

"I'll try to think of something," I told him.

What was I going to do?

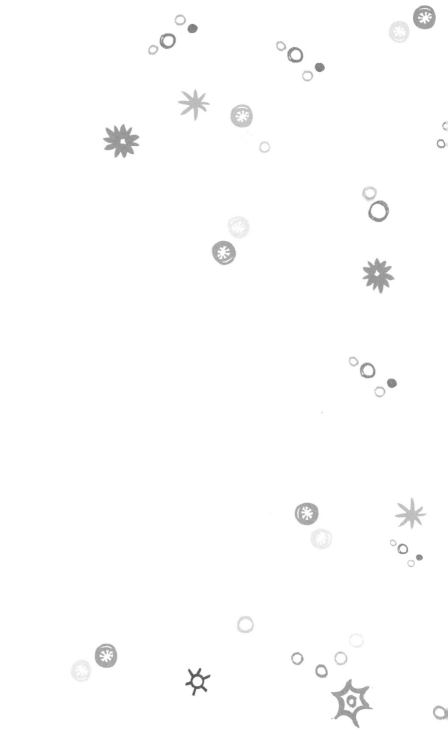

Chapter Fourteen

I swam quickly through the ocean, and even though I felt down about Owen's party, I couldn't help smiling at a group of lobsters and crabs who waved at me along the way. I really did love all the creatures in the sea, and they helped cheer me up.

The guards outside Neptunia nodded when I swam through the coral entrance. They were getting used to my coming and going.

When I darted inside the front door at home, Dad was sitting at the kitchen table.

"Rachel," he said. "Where were you?"

"Hi, Dad," I said. "I went to see Owen. I missed him more than I realized."

"I figured as much," he said. "But from now on, you need to let me know. I was getting worried."

"Sorry, Dad," I replied.

That's when I noticed a big cake sitting on the middle of the table. Thirteen unlit candles were stuck in the top.

"I feel terrible for messing up your birthday," he said. "I should have planned a party and had your friends over. I'm not as good at these things as your mom was."

"Well, I spent the day with my best friend, which made it great. Owen couldn't have come for a party anyway," I reminded him.

"I guess so." He patted my hand when I sat down beside him. "The Queen's cook made the cake when I told her it was your birthday. It's your favorite — shrimp-vanilla."

I didn't tell him that Owen's mom had made a cake too. And that it had been one of the most delicious ones I'd ever tasted.

He put his arm around me. "I'm sorry we didn't have a birthday celebration for you."

"It's okay, Dad. I had a great birthday. And I'd love a piece of cake," I said. Then I forced myself to eat a big piece even though I was already full.

* * *

The week flew by with lots of rehearsals and fun. Finally the night of the concert arrived. I was excited to sing, but I couldn't stop thinking about Owen and his party.

Shyanna had invited Cora and me to her house on Friday afternoon. Shyanna's mom made snacks while we got ready. I'd offered to help Shyanna braid her hair. She stared at my necklace as I braided the front of her hair.

"Hey! That's beautiful. Is that new? Where did you get it?" Shyanna asked.

"Um . . . I got it from a friend," I told her, and glanced at Cora.

Cora's hair was curled in beautiful waves, and she was glossing up her purple tail with fish oil. She wasn't paying attention to us.

"An old friend," I added quietly.

Shyanna's eyes opened as wide as sand dollars. "Owen?" she whispered, but she wasn't quiet enough.

Cora swam closer and stuck her face right up to mine. "Who's Owen? Is he your boyfriend?"

"No," I said, but my cheeks reddened like a lobster in boiling water. "I mean, he's a boy, and he's a friend. But he's not a boyfriend."

"Why did he buy you a necklace, then?" Cora asked, putting her hands on her hips.

"It was for my birthday," I said quietly. I moved behind Shyanna to admire my work.

Shyanna spun around. "Your birthday? When is your birthday?"

"It was last Friday," I admitted and patted her braided head. "Your hair is done," I told her. "It looks beautiful. It's your best look yet."

"You just had your birthday and you didn't tell us?" Shyanna said. She looked surprised, mad, hurt, and sad all at the same time. She knew my secret, so I was surprised by her reaction.

Cora flipped in semicircles. "You had your thirteenth birthday? You had a leg ceremony without us?" Her mouth hung open, and she looked hurt too.

Shyanna and I exchanged a look. "We'll make it up to her later," Shyanna said with fake enthusiasm. "Right now, we should practice our song!" She was trying to distract Cora. She belted out the first line of the song. I joined in, thankful when Cora stopped frowning and sang along with us.

"We're all ready to go!" Shyanna announced when we finished the song. She hurried us off to have snacks, and luckily, kept up the conversation about things other than my birthday until we left for the big concert.

When we arrived at the Royal Gardens, we all took a deep breath. It was transformed with a stage that looked like the inside of an oyster shell. Shiny colors and pearls were strung together and hung from a peach coral reef dripping with sea flowers. It was beautiful!

Other mermaids who'd been picked to sing with the Queen were fussing around behind the stage. Workers roamed around them, some carrying huge stage props. Somehow I got separated from Cora and Shyanna and was shoved into a tight space with a group of other mergirls from Neptunia. I recognized one mermaid named Regina. Shyanna had said she was the most popular girl in school.

Regina noticed me right away. "You're Mr. Marlin's daughter, aren't you? The Queen's new singing instructor?"

I nodded.

"I saw you sing in the twelve-year-old category at the Melody Pageant. You were really good," said one of the other mermaids.

"Thanks," I said and smiled at her.

Regina glared back at me. "When do you turn thirteen?" she asked, putting her hands on her hips.

"Um. I already did?" I said, wondering why she seemed mad at me. "Last Friday."

"But you never had a party?" asked Regina. "At least I never heard about it. And I hear about all the important parties in Neptunia."

"I had a party," I said right away. "It just wasn't in Neptunia."

"But how could you have your leg ceremony without Shyanna and Cora?" Regina asked. "I saw them at Walrus Waterpark last Friday. I thought they were your best friends. That seems . . . fishy."

My cheeks burned. I couldn't think of anything to say. I glanced around, wishing the workers would hurry up so I could get away. I wished Shyanna and Cora would appear to defend me and get Regina to go away. She was acting as if I'd done something wrong. I didn't even know her! I didn't know what her problem was.

Then Regina narrowed her eyes. "You know . . . my mom heard a rumor. A rumor about your mom," she said with a smug look on her face.

I sucked in a deep breath. Oh no. Was she going to start teasing me because my mom was human and I was half-human? Some mermaids didn't approve of humans who became a mermaid by magic.

"My mom was amazing," I said, swallowing a lump in my throat.

"Regina," the nice mermaid said. "Her mom died. Don't be mean."

Regina wrinkled up her nose and moved away from me as if I smelled like three-day-old fish fries. "I only hope the rumors about your mom aren't true." And with that, she turned her back on me.

The nice mermaid smiled weakly at me, but turned back to the group. "Remember my leg ceremony? Everyone said it was the best one ever!" Regina said to her friends as she flipped her hair and batted her long eyelashes.

The other mermaids looked guilty, but they nodded. Finally the workers cleared out of the way, and the group swam off, Regina in the lead.

Just then, Shyanna and Cora swam over.

"There you are!" Shyanna cried. "We've been looking everywhere for you. We're on in five minutes! Can you believe it?"

"Are you okay?" Cora asked, looking closer at me.

"I'm fine." I faked a smile.

"I saw Regina," Cora said. "Was she being mean?"

"No, I'm fine," I told them again.

They looked like they didn't believe me, but it was too complicated to explain since Cora didn't know the truth yet. I knew I had to tell her soon, but I was waiting for the right moment.

An event worker came along and hurried us to the stage, and then, before I knew it, we were performing our song. It sounded pretty great. I felt like I was in a dream the entire time we were singing. And before I knew it, we were done.

It went by so fast! All of our hard work and practice had paid off. It was amazing how much music could still make me feel better.

After we finished, Cora and Shyanna hurried out to the audience to watch the rest of the show and help with Cora's sisters.

"Want to come along?" Cora asked.

I shook my head. "I'm going to stay here in case my dad needs help."

That was partly true. But I also had a plan.

Regina swam by to go on stage and looked right at me. "She's not even a real mermaid," she whispered to a friend, and both girls turned away from me.

I glanced at my dad behind the curtains. He was beyond happy directing the show and was totally in his element. I looked at my phone.

I wanted to see Owen so badly! If I left right away, I could make it to his party and be back before anyone missed me.

My dad had told me a hundred times that I needed to tell him when I was going to land, but he was too busy to bother right then. Plus, he didn't even have to know. I would be back before he even noticed I was gone.

I swam out of the Royal Gardens, and then out of the kingdom and toward the shore. When I got to land and grew legs, I hurried up the beach toward Owen's house.

Before I even reached Owen's backyard, I could hear the party. Owen's house was lit up with glowing party lights. Happy noises floated through the air. I went to the front of the house and was about to ring the doorbell to join the party when I heard noises and shouts.

"Last one in is a rotten egg!" someone yelled.

The thundering army of kids sounded louder than a sea storm. Everyone was running out through the backyard toward the beach, all of them wearing bathing suits. Owen led the pack, laughing, with

Justin, Morgan, and Mitchel at his side as they raced to the water. My heart sank. I went to watch them, knowing I couldn't go see Owen now. It was too risky being so close to the water. If I got any salt water on me, my tail would reappear.

Instead, I went as close to the shore as I could and watched from the shadows.

Owen and his friends were having so much fun. Owen looked so happy. He didn't look like he missed me at all.

I went back to his house to leave him his present. I'd braided seaweed into a necklace and attached a real shark tooth. I left his gift at the front door and then headed down the street to a quiet beach. I leaped back in the water, feeling like I didn't belonged in either one of my worlds.

Chapter Fifteen

In the morning, I was tired from all my sneaking around. Dad had to go see the Queen early to review her performances, and he'd told me to sleep in. I stayed in bed all morning, but before lunch, the doorbell started ringing and didn't stop.

"Hey, Rachel, I know you're in there," a voice shouted from outside. "Let me in, lazy bones!"

With a big sigh, I got up and swam to the front door. When I opened it, my jaw dropped.

Shyanna floated on the front porch, holding a giant bouquet of balloons shaped like sea creatures in one hand and a starfish-shaped gift bag in the other hand.

"Happy belated birthday, sleepyhead!" she cried. "Cora and I got these for you. She wanted to come too, but her sisters are sick and her mom wouldn't let her leave."

My heart filled with happiness. "You look like a one-mermaid party pack!"

Shyanna laughed. "Are you going to let me in?'

"Oh!" I opened the door, and she handed me the balloons and gift as we went inside. "Thank you so much!" I said. I tied the balloons to a chair in the living room and put the gift down on the table.

"I still can't believe we missed your birthday!" Shyanna said.

"It's okay. I mean, turning thirteen is not as big as a deal for me, because I already have legs." I sat in the chair with the balloons and grinned. Shyanna sat across from me.

"Still . . . it was your birthday! Everyone deserves to feel extra special on her birthday," she said, clearly making a valid point.

"I went to see Owen," I told her. "His mom made me a cake. And his friends came over."

Shyanna clapped her hands together. "I'm glad. He seems like a good friend. I wish I could have come! Will you introduce me to Owen when I get my legs? I've never met a human before!"

Before I could answer, the doorbell rang. I got up and floated over to the door. When I opened it, Cora was flipping around in circles. She tackled me immediately, hugging me and giggling. "My mom let me come. My sisters are all sleeping!"

Cora swam inside and pulled me along behind her. "Yay!" she said when she saw the table. "You didn't open our present yet. Open it now! Open it!" she cried.

The girls spun around while I opened the bag and pulled out matching bracelets made of black pearls and braided seaweed. "One for each of us!" Cora said. "Friendship bracelets for forever friends!"

We all slipped them onto our wrists and held them out to admire them.

"They're beautiful," I said. "Thank you."

"So," Cora said. "I've been dying to know. Who's this Owen that you're so close with? You didn't think I would forget to ask you about him, did you?"

I glanced at Shyanna and then swam closer to Cora and took her hand. "I have a secret," I said. "Shyanna already knows because she caught me in the act, but I made her promise not to tell anyone."

Cora looked at me and then at Shyanna and then back at me, blinking. Waiting.

"I'm sorry I didn't tell you earlier. It's hard. I get teased," I said. "And I loved my mom so much, it's hard to talk about."

Cora grabbed my other hand. "What? What's wrong, Rachel?" Cora asked.

I took a deep breath and closed my eyes. "My mom was a human."

I waited for her to drop my hand or pull away in disgust or something.

"So?" she said.

I opened my eyes and started to laugh. "That's all you have to say? It means I'm half-human."

She let my hands go. "Oh. That doesn't matter at all." She opened her eyes wide and her mouth wider. "Wait. Does that mean you have legs? And that you can use them all the time?"

I nodded, and she stared at me without even blinking. "That is so cool," she said, in total awe. "It must be a romantic story, your mom and dad. Wouldn't it be amazing to fall in love with a human? How magical."

Shyanna cleared her throat, raised her eyebrows, and stared at me. I knew she was thinking about me and Owen.

"Stop looking at me like that, Shy. Owen and I are not in love," I told her. "We are just friends. Best friends — nothing more."

Cora looked back and forth between Shyanna and me. "Wait. What? Is this boyfriend of yours a human?" she asked me.

I touched the shell necklace Owen had given me. "A friend who's a boy. And yes. Owen is human. And he doesn't know I'm a mermaid."

"Wow!" Cora went to the table and sat across from Shyanna. "How did you meet a human?" They both stared at me, waiting for more information, I guess.

"Some of the mermaids from Caspian found out I was half-human, and they used to tease me. I went to land a lot to escape, and that's when I met Owen. At first, I was a little afraid of him, but he's so nice and adventurous. We quickly became best friends. I didn't have to worry about getting teased when I was with him. I used to visit him at least once a week, but I haven't been visiting as often since we moved to Neptunia."

"What's it like? To have a human as a friend?" Cora asked.

"He's great," I said. "He makes me feel like I matter, you know? I mean, he's like us. Only he doesn't get to enjoy the ocean like we do. I feel sad about that."

Shyanna and Cora nodded. I could tell they were both thinking how awful it would be not to enjoy the ocean like we were able to.

"The thing is, I've been away so much," I said. "I'm worried he's going to forget about me."

"He won't forget about you," Shyanna said, and Cora nodded in agreement.

"How could he?" Cora said.

"Thanks," I said, smiling and looking down at my friendship bracelet. "I got teased a lot in Caspian. The other mermaids were really mean. And Owen was so important to me. He still is. And the thing is, I think my secret is out again. I think one of the mermaids here knows about my mom."

"Who cares? The mermaids here won't tease you," Shyanna said confidently.

"I don't know," I said doubtfully. "The mermaid who hinted about it . . . she didn't seem too happy. I don't want everyone to look at me like I'm different. I hate being different."

"Who was it?" Cora asked, jumping up again. She had a hard time staying still.

"Regina," I said quietly.

"Regina Merrick? She can be really mean," Shyanna told me. "Was she being mean to you?"

Cora was pace-swimming around the room. I shrugged and looked away. "It doesn't matter. I'm tired of having to keep secrets from everyone," I said. "I hate hiding the fact that I'm a mermaid from Owen. It is awful. He is my best friend, and he has no idea what my real life is like."

"You're perfect," Cora said. "Just the way you are."

"I don't feel like it." I paused before I made my big announcement. The thing I'd been thinking about all night. "But I think I have a solution," I told them.

They both stared at me, waiting.

I stared back. Then, slowly, I said, "I think I might want to become human. All the time."

Chapter Sixteen

Silence.

Complete silence. That's the response I got from my big announcement.

"I've thought about it a lot," I told them, slowly swimming toward the table. "It's not an easy decision to make."

Shyanna and Cora both looked shell shocked.

"Why would you want to do that?" Cora asked quietly, frowning.

"It just seems easier," I said.

I plopped down in a chair, and we all faced each other in a circle. "You know how mermaid magic works," I said. "I would stay on land and not go near salt water for six months. After that, I would lose my tail. I could swim in the ocean, and it still wouldn't come back. And after I lost my tail, I would slowly start to forget that I'd ever been a mermaid. I would have memories of my life, of course, but it would all be kind of hazy. I'd believe I had always been human. End of story."

"You'd be willing to do that for a boy?" Cora asked, shocked.

"I wouldn't do this for a boy," I replied. "I would do this for me. I wouldn't have to feel like a freak anymore. I would be free from all the lies. I would be a normal person."

Shyanna started to cry. "But you would lose your beautiful tail," she said. "And what about all the wonderful parts of being a mermaid? What about exploring caves, looking for long-lost treasure? You'd never be able to talk to sea creatures again. And you would lose us."

"I would remember you," I said. "Just not all of it. And you could visit me once you have your legs."

Cora was up again, swim-pacing back and forth. "You wouldn't be able to race in the ocean. Or go to mermaid school or concerts. You wouldn't remember the King and Queen. You wouldn't remember the Melody Pageant. And what about your dad?"

I nodded. "I'd have to convince him to come with me. I could never leave him behind. I think he would do it. My mom was human. We could be too."

"I think that's about the saddest thing I've ever heard," said Shyanna. "We would miss you."

"You haven't even started school yet," Cora said softly. "And I really wanted you to join us on the Spirit Squad," she added. "But . . . it's also not right for mermaids to be sad."

Shyanna lifted her head to stare at Cora. "What are you saying, Cora?"

"I don't want her to leave," Cora said. Then she turned to me and asked, "But are you really that miserable and unhappy?"

I bit my lip and twirled my hair around my finger. "I love being a mermaid. And Neptunia is so wonderful. I'd miss you two so much." I paused, thinking how to say what I wanted to say. "It's just that . . . sometimes I feel left out . . . and so different from everyone else. And I'd really like to tell Owen the truth. He's always been honest with me, and he doesn't understand why I can't always be around. He was my first best friend."

"We're your best friends too," Shyanna said, her voice soft.

"I know. But Owen and I have a history. Like you two do," I explained.

"Being different isn't bad, you know," Shyanna said. "Who wants to be exactly the same as everyone else?" She was blinking fast, and her eyes were shiny with tears.

"Stay with us," she begged. "You'd be so unhappy never being a mermaid again. We'll come to shore with you as soon as we're thirteen. We can meet Owen when we get our legs. All of us can be friends. You can have both worlds if you stay with us. If you become human, that will be your only world."

Cora jumped up again. "We could make sure no one makes fun of you," she said.

I smiled at both of them. "You know I love you girls. But you can't always be around to protect me."

There was a noise from the front door. Dad swam inside. "Hey! Is there a party going on here without me?" He looked at Shyanna and Cora's faces. "Did I interrupt something? This looks like a serious party."

I glanced at my friends and shook my head slightly, pretending to zip up my lips so they'd know not to say anything.

"Not at all, Mr. Marlin!" Shyanna said. She tried to sound happy, but he frowned as if he suspected something was wrong.

"Listen, girls," he said. "The Queen wanted to let you know how thrilled she was with her concert — and you three, especially, for giving it such a good opening. She offered up her cook to make a special meal for us. Would you girls like to have dinner and then sleep over here with Rachel tomorrow night?"

Shyanna swam close and wrapped her arms around me tightly, hugging me like she'd never let go.

"We'd love to," Cora said, but her smile didn't last very long.

Dad frowned. He knew something was up.

Chapter Seventeen

After dinner, Dad sat down with me while I was putting clam juice in my hair to make it shine. "You wanted the girls to sleep over, didn't you?" he asked. "I thought it would be nice for you, but maybe I should have asked you first."

"Of course, Dad. It'll be great!" I ran my fingers through my hair to spread the juice around more evenly. "You know how much I love those girls. And having the Queen's cook make us dinner? Yummy!"

"I have a surprise before the girls come over," Dad said. "For the two of us. So don't make any plans."

"Okay!" I wasn't ready to have a serious talk

about becoming human yet, so I told him I was tired from all the concert excitement and went to my bedroom early that night.

I lay in my bed for a long time, staring up at my ceiling. The girls were seriously making me rethink my plan. I really did love being a mermaid. I loved the ocean and all the creatures, and I knew I'd miss everything I had to give up. Not only that, my dad would also have to give up the job he seemed to love so much.

The thing was, I suspected Regina was going to try to cause a lot of trouble for me. And I remembered all too well how hard it was to be made fun of all the time, especially when merkids also made fun of my mom. I missed her all the time, and I didn't care if she was part human or part penguin. I didn't want to hear anyone talking badly about her.

If only all the mermaids could accept me for who and what I was. I had Shyanna and Cora, but I'd always be the odd mermaid out. And what about

Owen? I didn't want to lose the first best friend I'd ever had.

I finally fell asleep, these thoughts drifting through my mind.

When I woke up in the morning, Dad was already gone. I played hide-and-seek with some clown fish in the morning, and in the afternoon, I played with some dolphins who came to visit. Life in the ocean really was magical. After a few more games, I headed home. Dad would be there soon. I had no idea what his surprise would be.

"We're going on an adventure, Rach!" Dad called when he finally got home from work. "You look like you need some cheering up, and I've been working far too much. Let's go have some fun! We both deserve it."

I nodded, trying not to look too guilty. I'd have to tell him my plans when we got home.

"I know you didn't get a big thirteen-year-old celebration like all the other mermaids, so we're going

167

to have our own celebration before dinner," he said, grinning. "You and I are going to sing with the whales!"

"Really?" I gasped. That had been our favorite thing to do before Mom died. We would travel outside Caspian and call to the whales. The whales didn't usually sing with other sea creatures, but they could never resist joining in when they heard Dad and me singing together. Dad had taught me how to harmonize with the whales in a special key.

We swam out of Neptunia and kept going, the two of us bouncing in and out of waves toward the deepest parts of the ocean. Once we were in whale territory, Dad started to sing in his glorious voice. He soon signaled for me to join him, and before I knew it, sea creatures from all depths of the ocean came to watch.

We sang and sang, and dolphins and sea turtles danced around Dad and me, clapping their fins along to the music! Finally, it was time to leave. We bid farewell to all of our new friends and began to swim

back toward Neptunia. On the way back, he stopped to show me a rare frost flower that only grows in the ocean.

"Is everything okay, Rachel?" Dad asked me when we got home. "I want you to be happy. If you don't like it here, we can move again."

"Oh, Dad," I said. My eyes stung, and I thought I might cry. "You love it here, don't you? Working with the Queen?"

He swam to me and put his arm around me. "The main reason we moved here was so you would be happier. That's the most important thing to me."

I leaned against him. "I love Neptunia, Dad. I really do," I said. "And Shyanna and Cora are the best. It's just . . ."

"What is it?" He stared down at me with concern.

"I miss Owen. I'm afraid he's forgetting about me. I can't go and see him as much as I once did," I explained. "He was — I mean, is — my best friend. I feel like I'm losing him."

Dad nodded. He was a great listener.

"And, well, one of the mermaids found out I'm half-human," I said. "I have no idea how, but I guess it doesn't matter. I'm afraid the teasing is going to start up again. I don't know if I'll ever fit in, no matter what kingdom we go to. When mermaids find out about Mom, some of them don't like it."

His face turned red. "Who said something?" he asked angrily. "I will talk to her parents."

"No, Dad. You know that will only make it worse," I said.

He let go of me and swam in a circle, flipping his tail in frustration. "But it's not right. There has to be something we can do."

"Well," I told him. "Maybe there is something. I've been thinking about it a lot."

He tilted his head, waiting.

"What if we became human?" I asked softly. "I mean . . . what if we went to live on land? Forever."

171

Chapter Eighteen

Dad gasped. "You don't want to be a mermaid anymore?"

"I love being a mermaid," I said. "But I'm sick of being different. If we became human together, we would eventually forget our mermaid life. We'd fit in with the humans, and I could still keep Shyanna and Rachel as friends. They could come visit once they get their legs. I wouldn't remember that they were mermaids, but we could still be friends. All four of us — Owen, Shyanna, Cora, and me."

"That's really what you want?" Dad asked.

I nodded. "It wouldn't be so bad, would it? I mean, you must know a lot about being human from being married to Mom."

He hugged me again. "Being different is what makes us special, Rach."

"Sometimes it's hard being special," I admitted.

Suddenly, the doorbell rang, interrupting us. Shyanna and Rachel were floating at the door, arriving for the sleepover party.

"I know that." Dad sighed, looking a little defeated. "I'll do anything for you, Rachel. You know that. Let me see what I can do."

* * *

"Wake up, girls!"

I rubbed my eyes and looked at the clock beside my bed. It was early! Why was Dad waking us up? Didn't he know we liked to stay up as late as we could keep our eyes open at sleepover parties? Shyanna and Rachel were still sleeping on the floor beside my bed.

"Up and at 'em!" Dad called.

We all groaned.

"Come on. I'll make sardine pancakes for breakfast, but you'll have to eat them quickly. In the meantime, comb your hair, brush your teeth, and get ready!"

"Ready for what?" I asked, groggily. "Dad, sleepover parties don't end at seven in the morning. We still have things to do. We haven't even painted our fingernails or braided shells into our hair."

He tried really hard without Mom, but sometimes Dad really didn't understand girl rules.

"This is important," he said. "I talked to the Queen last night."

The girls rubbed their eyes. I frowned, asking him, "You did? When?"

"When I took the cook home last night after dinner," he explained. "I asked the Queen for a

special meeting. She's a busy lady, and the only time she could meet with us was at eight this morning. So we have to get going. All of us! This is important. Lend the girls some sparkly tops and make sure you all look presentable."

Shyanna and Cora nodded, excited. It wasn't often that mermaids our age got to meet with the Queen in private.

"What's it about?" I asked him, glancing at my two friends, who looked equally puzzled.

"It's a secret." He wouldn't say anything more.

The girls and I jumped up out of bed and started to get ready while Dad made breakfast.

"I wonder what your dad is up to," Shyanna whispered.

I squeezed her hand. "I have no idea," I said. "All I know is that I'm sick of secrets."

Chapter Nineteen

The King and Queen's palace was so fancy! It was hard to believe Dad got to go there every day for work. Shyanna, Cora, and I giggled when the Queen's guard announced our names outside the private quarters. We tried our hardest not to freak out when they led us into the Queen's parlor.

The Queen was sitting on her throne, wearing a light purple cape. Her long blond hair was braided with sparkles and the fanciest pearls. She looked regal, proper, and perfect.

She stood and winked at us when we came in. "Look. It's my favorite warm-up singers and my coach!" she said. The nerves in my stomach melted. "You girls did such an amazing job at the concert. I'd like to do it again sometime!"

The Queen offered us some tea, and we sat at a table in front of her throne. There were large cookies with pink frosting on a plate on the table. It might have been early, but that didn't stop Shyanna from grabbing a cookie right away.

"Your majesty," my dad said, bowing his head. "I asked to speak with you today about a matter of extreme importance."

We all stared at Dad.

"As you know, my daughter, Rachel, is half-human," he continued.

"I am aware," the Queen said with a smile. "Her mother — your wife — was a wonderful mermaid, wife, mom, and friend. She took to our life so well. It was a pleasure to welcome her to our world with

magic. It was one of the best decisions I have ever made. I am still so sorry for your loss."

"Thank you. We are too. We miss her every day," Dad said, looking down. Then he glanced at me. "This is what I came to discuss. The fact is that no recent mermaids in Neptunia have had human mothers. And in the past — in other kingdoms — Rachel has been teased for being half-human."

Cora and Shyanna each grabbed one of my hands and squeezed it tightly.

The Queen frowned, but my dad kept going. "Rachel can travel to land and stay there as long as she wants. I've allowed her to explore, and while on land she made a really special friend. A human."

The Queen nodded. "Owen," she said. "He is a good human."

My cheeks got a little warm.

"Don't look so surprised, Rachel," the Queen said. "We know about Owen. For your protection. We keep an eye on our mermaids, even when they're on land."

"Unfortunately," Dad said, "teasing is something Rachel never escapes. For that, among other reasons, she's expressed interest in becoming a human."

The Queen tilted her head and gazed at me with wide, sympathetic eyes. "Is that true?"

I nodded, unable to speak. Afraid.

"If you give up your tail, you can never get it back," the Queen said.

I swallowed, grateful the girls were holding my hands. I didn't want to think about giving up being a mermaid forever, but it seemed like the best solution. I wanted Owen to be a part of my life all the time. I wanted to have a normal life.

"I have a different solution," my dad said. "One that might make Rachel reconsider her choice."

We all stared at him. Even the Queen.

"What if we grant Owen temporary merman status to visit Rachel? He's thirteen, so he could do the same as mermaids do on land, only in reverse. A few hours in the ocean to see her life. And then

Rachel could share her friends and her world here with Owen. She wouldn't have to keep her real self a secret from him anymore."

"Exposure to humans is always risky," the Queen said, frowning.

"But my mom proved to be trustworthy!" I cried.

She raised her hand. "Let me finish, please."

I pressed my lips tightly.

"Owen has the right human qualities to be trusted," the Queen continued. "The question is, would having Owen visit keep you from wanting to turn to human form permanently?"

I nodded my head vigorously. Having Owen know the truth really would help. My dad was a genius.

"He would have to keep the secret," the Queen said. "And if he didn't, he would turn into a merman. He would never be able to return back to human form. His family would believe he was lost at sea. This is a delicate matter that must be taken very seriously. Do you understand what you are asking?"

I thought about Owen and how he always said there was nothing that could prevent him from being my friend. I knew he could be trusted. I nodded again.

"I do, and I know they are only teenagers," my dad said. "But I believe they have old souls and can be trusted. Their friendship is stronger than any I've ever witnessed."

The Queen sipped her tea and then put down her cup. "From what I've seen, I agree with your assessment. Their bond is incredible."

"Sometimes a strong friendship can be as strong as love," my dad said. "Wouldn't you agree, Queen?"

"I do. I really do," she said with a smile. "Rachel, you may tell Owen the truth. He can be brought here if he agrees. It is his choice. If he doesn't agree, he will forget what you've told him."

"Really?" I whispered. I was in shock.

"Once you tell him," the Queen explained, "you must be aware that if chooses not to be part merman, you will no longer be allowed to visit him. Too much exposure after that may wear off the mermaid magic, and he could eventually remember the truth about you. That cannot be allowed to happen."

I loved being a mermaid far too much to give it up. I knew in my heart that being different didn't mean being bad. If I could tell my best friend the truth and bring him to Neptunia to see my life here, it would be worth all the hassle. I was sure he wouldn't turn me down. I was so sure, I was willing to risk losing him forever.

I would tell Owen the truth and offer him a chance to see a life that other humans couldn't even imagine. The world beneath the sea. Having the four of us together would be a dream come true. Owen, Shyanna, Cora, and me!

I gulped and nodded at the queen. She snapped her finger, and a mermaid appeared and gave me a magic pill. It would turn Owen into a merman.

If he chose to be one.

Chapter Twenty

The next morning, Shyanna, Cora, and my dad each hugged me before I left to find Owen. I was beyond nervous. I couldn't believe it was really happening! It was like a dream.

I found Owen on shore in our special spot. I had sent Owen a text the night before, so I knew he'd be waiting for me. I didn't know how to tell him my secret, so I just blurted it out. When I finished telling him the truth, and the rules about knowing the truth and the choice he had to make, he didn't look upset at all. He didn't even look that surprised. I guess that is a normal boy response to most things.

"Mermaids," he said, smiling. "That's the coolest thing I've ever heard."

"You aren't mad or weirded out?" I asked.

"It's weird, but I always knew there was something different about you. Not weird different, but magical different."

"You did?" I asked.

"I think that's what brought us together. And of course I can keep it a secret. You're my best friend. And of course I want to see your world!"

My cheeks glowed with happiness. He looked back at me, and I saw that his cheeks were glowing too. He touched his neck, and I noticed he was wearing the shark tooth necklace I got him for his birthday. I touched the shell necklace he gave me, the one that I never took off.

For a moment I wondered if we'd ever be more than friends, but then I tucked that idea away. I didn't want to ruin what we had right now. A great friendship was more than I could ask for.

"Merpeople," he said as we walked toward the ocean. "I always wondered why you were constantly on the beach, but you would never swim." He pointed at my legs. "I can't wait to see your tail!"

"I can't wait to see yours!" I told him, and we both stared down at his legs.

"Me neither!" he yelled, and then he started to run toward the water.

"Wait!" I called and laughed.

"You have to take this first," I said as I pulled out the magic pill the Queen gave me. "You are sure about all of this? You don't need to think about it longer or anything?"

He nodded. "Are you crazy? I can't wait!"

"Okay. Then take this, and we'll go to Neptunia to meet my friends," I said.

He swallowed the pill. "Tastes like fish," he said, smiling. He stared down at his legs, waiting.

I laughed and pulled him into the ocean. My tail spread down, shimmering in the sunshine.

"Wow!" he said, his eyes sparkling in amazement.

And then we both watched as his tail spread down until his legs disappeared and a tail took their place. It was a glorious tail, reds and oranges twinkling in the water. He whooped loudly, and then we dove down under a wave. The grin didn't leave his face. He was an amazing swimmer and took to his fins right away.

Owen was like a little kid, stopping to admire every shellfish and jellyfish and waving lobster. He played with the dolphins that came to greet us, and the grumpy old whale that swam by and blew a spout of water made him laugh.

When we finally arrived at Neptunia, Shyanna and Cora were waiting in Walrus Waterpark for us. They looked as happy as me and Owen. The girls hugged Owen like he was an old friend. And it was then I knew that this was the right choice.

But soon, we weren't the only merpeople at Walrus Waterpark. Regina and a group of her mermaid friends arrived.

"Who is this?" Regina asked, swimming closer.

"I'm Owen," he said, not intimidated. "And this is my best friend, Rachel, and my new friends Shyanna and Cora. We're merpeople!"

We all laughed at his enthusiasm.

"I know what we are," Regina said, turning her nose up a bit. But he also intrigued her, I could tell. "Where did you come from?"

He winked at her. "That's kind of a secret between friends. Do you mind?" he asked, and then he twirled up and did a double flip turn. "I have to say, I like Neptunia a lot. You'd better get used to seeing me around."

Regina was not smiling. I had a feeling I was going to have to deal with her a lot once school started, but I didn't care. Having Owen here was worth dealing with Regina.

She swam away, with her friends following behind. I grabbed Owen's hand. His time was almost up already, and we had to get him back to land. "Come on, Owen, we have to get going," I said.

"We're so glad we got to meet you!" Shyanna said.

"And we'll come visit you on shore once we turn thirteen and get our legs!" Cora added.

We were all excited to add a fourth best friend to our friendship circle. "Come on, Owen," I said to him. "Let's go to shore. You can come back and visit soon!"

"Just try to keep me away," he said.

Part Three: Cora's Tale

Chapter Twenty-One

It didn't matter how much fun summer break was. The first day back to school was always really exciting. Sure, I was nervous for school to start again. But I was more excited than nervous.

I couldn't wait to find out what teacher I would have. I was hoping that my best friends Rachel and Shyanna would be in the same class as me. I could survive without them, but it definitely wouldn't be as fun. When school started, I wouldn't have to babysit my sisters all day, which was a huge bonus.

Plus, this was a big year for me. It was the first year I'd be able to audition for the Neptunia Spirit Squad. The Spirit Squad is an important part of each kingdom. The team attends school and community events, bringing a fun dynamic through dancing, singing, and cheering. Once you are on the team, you are a part of it for life!

I'd dreamed about being on the team since I was a baby, when Mom would tell me stories about being on the team. These days, my mom was so busy with my sisters that sometimes it felt like she's forgotten about me. Being on the Spirit Squad would definitely make her notice me!

On the morning of the first day of school, my little sisters helped me decide what to wear. I couldn't decide which top screamed Spirit Squad Member. I narrowed it down to a new purple one and my favorite light blue one. When I came out of the bathroom in my new purple top, my sisters clapped and yelled. It was clearly the winner.

Sometimes I complained about how loud my sisters were, but I liked having them around when I needed a cheering section. They really could be sweet sometimes.

"Cora! Rachel and Shyanna are here," my mom called to me.

"Just in time," I said.

"Bye, Cora! Have fun! Good luck with your classes!" my mom shouted as she tucked Jewel under one arm and chased Pearl and Ruby down the hall. Sweet or not, those girls were a lot of work!

"Bye!" I called to my sisters and my mom, even though I knew they weren't listening.

"Wow!" Shyanna said. "That purple top really pops on you!"

"Thanks." We raved about each other's outfits. I admired Rachel's curly red hair and Shyanna's braids. The three of us linked arms and started swimming toward the school. Luckily I lived pretty close, which is why we all met up at my place.

"I'm really nervous," Rachel said as we approached the front of the school. I wasn't surprised that Rachel was nervous. She moved to Neptunia over the summer, and being the new girl was tough. Plus, it made me feel better that I wasn't the only nervous one.

"Don't worry, we've got your tail," Shyanna said.

"It's my legs I'm more worried about," Rachel joked, trying to relieve some tension.

Rachel was half-human, which was a big secret. She didn't want any of the kids to find out and bully her. She'd had some problems at her old school, so it made sense that she would hide her secret.

Shy and I were excited to catch up with our school friends and to introduce them to Rachel. We knew they were going to love her as much as we did. We reached the school and stopped to admire the giant statue of the school's founding mermaid, Michelle, at the school entrance. We showed Rachel how to rub Michelle's fin for luck.

"Everyone's going to love you just the way you are," I told her. I didn't think anyone would care that she was half-human, except maybe to think it was super cool that she could go on land whenever she wanted and for as long as she wanted.

We swam together through the pillars of old white coral that led into the school grounds. It was chaotic inside. Merboys and mergirls of all ages were doing flips and mingling and waving at each other.

"Hi!" I yelled to Cassie Shores as she swam by with a group of mergirls. She was one of the most popular mermaids at school and was also on the swim team with me last year. Like me, she was excited that this year we were eligible to try out for the Spirit Squad.

"She's a shoo-in for the Spirit Squad," I told Rachel. "She composes songs, and she's amazing at it. Making the Spirit Squad will be a great way for you to get to know her too!"

"Cool," Rachel said. "If you like her, so will I."

"She's as obsessed as Cora about being on the Spirit Squad," Shyanna said.

"I wouldn't say obsessed," Cora said.

"I would!" Shyanna winked to let me know it was okay, but Rachel wasn't paying attention. Instead, she was looking at a group of mermaids swimming by.

"That's the girl who said things about my mom during the Neptunia talent show," Rachel whispered to us.

"That's Regina," Shyanna said. "She's not the nicest mermaid."

"That is a huge understatement! She is just mean," I said as I glanced at Regina and frowned.

I needed to show positive behavior since the Spirit Squad selections were coming up, but it wasn't always easy.

Chapter Twenty-Two

I didn't have long to dwell on Regina and her mean ways because Principal Tetra's voice boomed over the PA system. "Attention, everyone. Please report to the Dolphin Gymnasium. We are ready to announce class placements for this school year. Also, we have a special surprise this morning."

A special announcement? That sounded like a great way to start the school year!

We joined the crowd of merkids swimming into the gymnasium. Everyone was whispering and pointing, and I certainly understood why when I saw who was on the stage.

"That's the King and Queen!" Shyanna whispered, but it was pretty obvious. They were wearing crowns and were so regal looking with their shiny hair and sparkling tails. They were a beautiful couple!

Our principal stood on the stage. "Welcome back, everyone! Before the King and Queen make their special announcement, I am going to read the list of class assignments for the year. Please settle down and listen closely."

It took a couple of minutes to get all the merkids organized. Rachel, Shyanna, and I stuck together. Rachel was gripping our hands so tightly it hurt. She was also looking a little panicked. Since she was new at school, she was a little nervous about everything. I smiled to show her that we were all in this together.

As the principal read name after name, I was getting even more hopeful that the three of us would be in class together. And guess what? That's exactly what happened! Shyanna, Rachel, and I were in Ms. Swift's class list together!

Once the excitement of class assignments died down, Principal Tetra announced the King and Queen. The entire crowd went quiet as the pair stood and moved to the front of the stage.

"As you all know, this is the one-hundredth anniversary of Mermaid Kingdom," the King said. "To celebrate, there will be a Mermaid Kingdom Festival, including a special competition between individual kingdoms."

"Merkids from each kingdom will form teams to compete in a series of special spirit competitions, including singing, dancing, and chanting or cheering," the Queen announced. "We want to wish the merkids of Neptunia good luck!"

"The team that shows the best teamwork throughout the competition will win a trophy and a big donation for their kingdom and school," the King added.

A cheer rose from the merkids gathered in the gym. I couldn't believe this was happening! Since it was the one-hundredth anniversary of Mermaid Kingdom, being on the Spirit Squad was even more important than ever!

The Queen raised her hand again. "Earlier today, we picked the team leader for Neptunia. Based on community involvement and outstanding school achievements, Regina Merrick is your team leader."

As Regina, with a smug look on her face, confidently waved at everyone, there were polite claps. There were more groans than cheers.

I was really hoping Cassie would get to be the team leader, as she was nice, fair, and talented. There wasn't anything I could do about it now but politely clap and deal with it.

Principal Tetra congratulated Regina, thanked the Queen and King for their appearance, and dismissed us to our classrooms. The chaos and noise quickly returned as we swam out of the gym.

"Are you nervous about trying out for the Spirit Squad?" I asked Rachel.

She bit her lip and nodded. "I don't think Regina likes me very much."

"Regina doesn't like many people," Shyanna said.

"Don't worry about her!" I said with a smile. "With your voice, you're perfect for the team! You may be new, but you've already been noticed."

Shyanna looked at me and then back at Rachel. "Maybe Rachel doesn't want to be on the Neptunia Spirit Squad," she said.

"What? That's crazy!" I said. I couldn't even imagine not wanting to be on the team.

"That's not it. I'm just nervous," Rachel said.

"Me too!" I told her.

"I don't know why you're so nervous, Cora," Shyanna said. "You are super athletic and everyone likes you. Plus, you have a great attitude about everything, which is rare."

"Thank you, Shy," I said, blushing a little.

"You're perfect for the Neptunia team, just like your mom was," Shyanna said as she turned to Rachel. "Cora's mom was on the Neptunia Spirit Squad for the seventy-fifth anniversary of Mermaid Kingdom. She helped bring the trophy to Neptunia."

"I want to start practicing right away," I said. "Can we practice at your cave, Rachel? My sisters will be in the way at mine."

"Sure!" Rachel said. "Maybe my dad can even help us with a new song."

"Awesome! We really can't get better help than the music instructor for the Queen!" I said.

"See? Just because Regina is in charge doesn't mean we can't have fun, right?" Shyanna said.

I nodded, thankful. What would I do without my friends?

Chapter Twenty-Three

By the end of the week, I was in full school mode. The school year was going pretty great. I loved Ms. Swift. We were studying shipwrecks in sea studies, and we even went on a field trip to explore an old sunken ship. Ms. Swift always let Rachel and Shyanna and me work together. The only thing that made my heart feel sad was that Rachel seemed so different at school. At school, Rachel was really quiet and reserved. Shyanna and I did everything we could to involve her, but it didn't help.

There was nothing wrong with being shy, but that wasn't the real Rachel. When she was with me and Shyanna alone, she was so full of spark and energy. But at school, she was so worried about the other mermaids finding out her secret that she barely talked at all. It made me sad. I could not imagine trying to be someone else all day just to fit in!

Rachel thought the merkids wouldn't want to be friends with her if they knew she was half-human. I knew Cassie and her group of friends would accept Rachel no matter what. They were cool girls. They knew what was really important in life.

I told Rachel she should be proud and announce it at the top of her lungs, but Shyanna explained to me that Rachel needed to do things her own way.

I had to stop focusing on Rachel and focus on tryouts for the Spirit Squad. My plan was to practice every day after school, but getting together with Shyanna and Rachel was harder than breaking open an oyster shell.

Because of the special anniversary this year, the tryouts were moved up and were less than a week away. They wanted to give the Spirit Squad more time to practice as a team.

Every time Rachel, Shyanna, and I scheduled an after-school practice, it seemed like there would be some sort of family emergency. First, Pearl got sick and I had to look after Jewel while my mom was at the doctor. Then, Jewel ripped her tail and needed stitches, so I had to babysit again. Just when everything seemed fine, Ruby got the flu and Mom made me stay home and help. Those three girls sure were a handful!

I often envied the quiet of being an only child, like Shyanna and Rachel. The two of them were getting in lots of practice time at Rachel's, and they didn't even need it.

I hated missing the practice time with the girls. I also hated missing out on the fun. Besides, Rachel's dad was the Queen's singing coach.

Fortunately, my sisters, my cousin Shelby, and my parents liked to watch me perform. They helped by singing Rachel and Shyanna's parts when I was practicing. I had my moves down, but I still wasn't confident about my singing. I knew Rachel and Shyanna would make the Spirit Squad because their voices were so amazing. My plan was to distract the judges from my singing voice by dancing my heart out. I could sing, but it wasn't my best talent. I could do decent harmonies, but I was no power singer like my friends.

But that wasn't going to stop me. I wasn't going to let anything stand in the way of making the Spirit Squad. I had been dreaming about this for too long to give up. All I could do was work hard and try my best. That had to count for something, right?

Chapter Twenty-Four

Finally, the day for the tryouts arrived. Rachel, Shyanna, and I wore matching pink tops and pink nail polish. Shy's mom even made us matching braided sea flower tiaras.

Before our performance, the three of us put our heads together. "Let's do this, girls!" I told them. We swished our tails together, and then the music for our number started.

What happened next was kind of a blur. I know I hit all of my notes, and Shyanna and Rachel sang like angels. As for the dancing, we nailed it! We were in perfect unison, and each solo was unique and energetic. Afterward, I was so relieved to be done I could barely talk. We stayed to watch the other performers. I was impressed. Everyone did an incredible job, and with that kind of competition, I knew it was going to be tough to make the team.

When all the performers finished, Principal Tetra announced that the judges would go and vote. The judges were former members of the Spirit Squad. Since Regina was the team leader, she got to make all the final decisions.

I bit all the glittery nail polish off my nails waiting for the committee to return with the results. The water in the gym seemed electric, and everyone was bursting with excitement. Finally the committee members swam back inside, led by Regina. I felt positively seasick.

"Don't worry, Cora," Rachel whispered calmly. "You're going to make the team. I know it."

"The results are in," the principal announced. "The Spirit Squad members have been selected.

Thank you to every mermaid and merboy who tried out for the Spirit Squad. You made the decision particularly difficult."

My breath was coming fast. Shyanna took my other hand as Regina stepped forward. She smiled with her pearly white teeth.

Rachel took a deep, nervous breath. It was my turn to squeeze her hand. "You were great," I whispered to her.

Rachel nodded, but her lips were one thin line again. She looked a little pale as well.

"The first member of the Spirit Squad," Regina announced, "is Shyanna Angler."

Everyone went crazy clapping and cheering. I screamed so loud I almost passed out. Shyanna grinned and swam to the front. A few more names were called; most of them were mermaids I knew and had been positive would make the team.

Regina announced a few more names, including Cassie. We all cheered extra loud for her. No matter how much I wanted to make the squad, I knew Cassie wanted it just as much.

I closed my eyes and refused to count how many spots were left. Instead, I started making promises inside my head. If I made the team, I would never complain about my sisters again. I would always eat my krill and never make fun of snails racing again.

"And now," Regina dramatically shouted, "the final Spirit Squad member." Every merkid in the entire gymnasium seemed to be holding their breaths. "Last, but certainly not least, the final member of the Neptunia Spirit Squad is . . ." Regina cleared her throat and paused.

"Cora Bass."

My entire body whooshed with relief. A grin took over my face. But then I looked beside me and my grin disappeared.

Rachel.

Rachel hadn't made the team.

Chapter Twenty-Five

It didn't make sense. The judges hadn't chosen Rachel? But she was one of the best singers, not only in Neptunia, but in the entire Mermaid Kingdom. I couldn't believe she hadn't made the team!

"Don't be sad for me," Rachel said. "Go on up there and celebrate. You deserve this!"

She pushed me forward, cheering the entire time. When I got to the front, Shyanna tackled me with a giant hug. We did a somersault together and stopped at exactly the same time. When we looked out into the crowd at Rachel, she smiled brightly and gave us a big thumbs-up.

"I can't believe she didn't make it," I said to Shyanna.

"I know!" she answered.

The committee made some announcements, and then it was done. We swam back to Rachel. "Don't feel bad for me," she told us as soon as we reached her. "I'm okay. I'm more than happy to help coach you two. I'm pretty good at coaching from watching my dad teach."

We pulled her in for a group hug. When we let go, she blinked fast and smiled, but I saw a lone tear escape from her eye.

* * *

"That was a really great practice," Cassie said to me and Shyanna. It was fun spending more time with Cassie again. She was just as smart, funny, and kind as I remembered.

"Well, except when Regina said she had to leave early," Shyanna said, "and you offered to take over the practice. I thought she was going to have a temper tantrum, but you still insisted. I couldn't believe you did that."

I grinned. Shyanna didn't like conflict. As a big sister, I had lots of experience with it. "Nah. She was fine."

Cassie laughed. "Only because you didn't really give her a choice."

I shrugged. Regina could be mean sometimes, but I didn't let her get to me. She was just another mermaid. I didn't have time to worry about her.

"You did a really great job leading our group," Shy said.

"I guess being bossy comes naturally to me," I said.

Shyanna shook her head. "No. It's not being bossy. It's being a good leader. After Regina left and you took over, we were a completely different squad.

We worked together so much better, which is what we need to do to win this thing."

"You're good at motivating, which is a big role for the team leader," Cassie chimed in.

"Thanks," I said, blushing. I tried to hide my proud smile, but my heart grew a few sizes. "Regina is a really good dancer and singer, though."

"But she isn't a very good leader," Shyanna replied, making a good point.

"She tries," I said. I didn't want to talk about it anymore, even though I kind of agreed with her that Regina wasn't always the best at leading the group.

I didn't want to admit it to anyone, even Shy, but I'd lost some of my excitement about being on the Spirit Squad. The fact that Rachel hadn't been selected still bothered me. Not just because she was a great friend — fair was fair — but because she was a great performer. I suspected that Regina maybe did have something against Rachel, and I needed to get to the bottom of it.

"Hey," I said. "My mom isn't expecting me to be home to babysit for another hour. Let's go to Rachel's and see how she's doing. We've been so busy with Spirit Squad lately that we haven't seen much of her."

"That's a great idea," Shyanna said.

"This is my cue to head home," Cassie said.

"Are you sure?" I asked. "You are more than welcome to come with us."

"I don't think Rachel would like that very much. I get it, though," she said. "Being the new girl is tough."

"Some other time," Shyanna agreed.

We each gave Cassie a hug and swam fast to see Rachel, swirling with excitement as we made our way over to Rachel's cave in the new part of Neptunia.

We swam up to the front door and rang the bell, but no one answered. We looked at each other.

"She's not home," I said.

"I wonder where she went," Shyanna said.

"She's probably helping her dad. Let's wait. I bet they'll be home soon," I said, hoping I was right.

We played with some sea turtles and chased after some cute baby crabs who were playing hide-and-seek. Finally, Rachel swam into view.

"There you are! Finally!" Shyanna said. "Where's your dad?"

"My dad?" she said.

"Weren't you helping him?" Shy asked.

Rachel smiled. "No. He's with the Queen. She's working on a new performance and needed his help." She swam to her cave and waited for us to follow.

Shyanna and I exchanged a quick glance as we followed her into the living room. "So where were you?" I asked, even though I could guess.

"I went to visit Owen." She swam over and stretched out on a hammock, looking very pleased with herself.

Owen was Rachel's best friend, a human she'd met on land. He'd recently been granted magical merman powers to visit us in Mermaid Kingdom for two hours at a time, but it was easier for Rachel to visit him on land. Shyanna and I looked at each other again, and her worried expression echoed how I felt. Not so long ago, Rachel had been thinking about leaving Mermaid Kingdom to become human. What if she still wanted to?

"Why don't you bring him here?" I asked Rachel.

"I would rather go on land," she said and got up from the hammock. "Legs are restricting in the water, but they're kind of fun on land. I'm learning how to run faster. It's pretty amazing."

Shy and I sat on the lumpy couch made of seaweed and sea sponges. "You're sure you're okay?" I asked again. "You're not thinking about becoming human again, are you?"

Rachel shook her head and her red hair flowed out behind her. "Don't look so worried, you two. I'm fine. Really."

"We're your best friends," I said. "You can tell us anything."

Rachel swam back to the hammock and sat.

"Well," she finally said, "maybe I feel a little left out because you two are so busy after school with practice. But it's okay. I don't want you to feel bad. I want you to do great at the Spirit Games."

We swam over and hugged her tight.

When we let go, she sniffled. "Maybe I'm a little scared you two are going to forget about me and things will be like they were in Caspian. I was so lonely there, and people made fun of me for being half-human. It was terrible."

"That's when you started hanging out with Owen, right?" Shy asked.

"Yes," Rachel said. "I don't know what I would have done without him."

"I hate that the Spirit Squad is making you feel so bad," I said. "It's supposed to make everyone happy, and I don't want to be a part of something that makes you miserable."

"I agree," Shyanna said. "We don't need to be a part of the Spirit Squad."

Rachel shook her head hard. "No. No way. I know how important this is to you two — especially you, Cora. I'm not letting you quit because of me. I'm fine."

"It *was* important to me, but our friendship is way more important," I said. "Besides, we don't have practice tomorrow, so we definitely need to hang out."

My phone rang then. It was my mom, telling me to come home. "We'll see you after school tomorrow, okay?" I told Rachel.

She smiled and nodded, but the smile didn't reach her eyes. That didn't make me feel any better.

I had to fix it. I just wasn't sure how.

Chapter Twenty-Six

Before school the next day, Regina called a special meeting for the Spirit Squad. "The first competition will take place in ten days," she announced. "The contest will be at Caspian Castle, during the senior swim competition. Spirit Squads will perform between races. We need to win this and get off to a good start."

Everyone cheered and clapped.

"In preparation, we're going to have a special rehearsal after school today," Regina said.

My mouth dropped open. We'd promised Rachel we would be free to see her, but we really couldn't skip practice. Shy and I swam to find her and tell her the bad news.

"It's okay," Rachel said, smiling. "Don't look so guilty. It's exciting. I can't wait for the competition!"

The school day zipped past, and then the Spirit Squad gathered in the gym for our rehearsal. We lined up and started the routine.

My flips had really improved, and everything was going great, until the last part of the mermaid song. I opened my mouth to sing, but instead of a clear note, a horrible screech came out. It was so off key that everyone turned and looked at me. The music stopped playing. My face burned, and I covered my mouth with my hand. Regina put her hands on her hips and narrowed her eyes.

"Cora, what is wrong with you?" she said.

Everyone stared. My cheeks burned with humiliation, and my eyes filled with tears.

Shyanna swam close and patted my shoulder. "Don't worry about it. Just practice that note at home," she whispered. "You'll get it right."

We started again from the top. I fumbled through the song, singing really softly in case my voice cracked again. Regina did not look happy.

Shyanna and I swam home together, but after she left me to swim to her own cave, Regina swam up beside me. She must have been following us.

"Cora, you're the weakest link on our team," she told me. "We don't want to lose because of you. If you don't think you can hit that note properly, it would be better for everyone if you dropped out now."

I didn't want to let everyone down with my voice, but I wanted to be on the Spirit Squad more than anything. I shook my head.

"I won't mess up," I told her.

She glared at me and then nodded. "Please don't. We're having a full dress rehearsal tomorrow. You had better prove that you can do it."

With a flick of her tail, she swam away. I went inside my cave and immediately got swarmed by my sisters, who were arguing over a necklace of woven seaweed. I tried to shake off my gloom, but the tears came hard and fast.

Mom came into the room and swam to me. "Cora? Is everything okay?" She touched my forehead to see if I was warm. I wanted to tell her why I was upset, but she had enough to deal with all of my little sisters. I also didn't want her to know that the Spirit Squad wasn't perfect.

Just then, the doorbell rang.

"I'm fine, Mom. I'm just tired," I said. I fake smiled and went to answer the door. It was Rachel!

"You hang out with your friend," Mom said to me. "I've got the girls."

Rachel and I swam to my room. "Are you okay?" she asked. "I was coming home from visiting Owen and I saw you and Regina talking. It didn't look like a pleasant conversation."

I told her what Regina had said.

Rachel looked really mad. "Don't worry, Cora," she said. "I've got something that will help you."

Rachel asked my mom if I could go home with her. Mom let me go without even thinking about it. She knew something was wrong.

At her cave, Rachel dragged me inside her dad's room, which seemed really weird.

"Are we supposed to be in here?" I asked.

"It's okay. My dad keeps something of mine in his closet, but I'm allowed to take it out or use it anytime I want," Rachel said confidently.

She swam to the closet, but I floated by the doorway. Rachel took something out and turned, hiding it behind her back. She smiled. "You're not allowed to say no."

Then she pulled out the most beautiful mermaid top I'd ever seen. It sparkled with every color under the ocean with a shimmery, magical quality. It literally took my breath away.

"I want you to wear this. It was my mom's. The Queen gave it to her as a special gift when she married my dad. It's magical."

"Really?" I said, not fully believing her. "I think I need more than magic to help me be a better singer."

"Well, it helped my mom sing as charmingly and skillfully as a full-fledged mermaid," Rachel said. "Don't you think some magic had to be involved? She was a human!"

I stared at the shell top, completely amazed by how beautiful it was. Maybe it was magic!

"Oh, Rachel," I said, almost in shock. "I can't wear that. I'd be scared I'd ruin it or something. It's too much."

Rachel shook her head. "You are one of the most kind and responsible mermaids I've ever known. And you and Shyanna have made my life in Neptunia incredibly wonderful. I insist that you borrow it. I have complete trust in you. The magic will give you courage to perform as well as I know you can.

You only have to believe in yourself, as much as you believe in everyone else around you."

I didn't even know what to say. Rachel was amazing! She was willing to help me and our team even though Regina hadn't picked her.

Rachel held out the top and slipped out of the room so I could try it on. When I swam out wearing it, Rachel clapped and whistled.

"Wow!" Rachel said with a huge smile on her face. "It's perfect on you. I mean it! It was meant to be worn by you. My dad will be so proud to see you perform with it on."

"Are you sure?" I asked. I loved the top. Just the thought of wearing it made me believe I could sing better. "I feel so bad, Rachel. You're a gifted singer. You should be on the Spirit Squad. Not me."

Rachel shook her head. "No, really. Your voice is great, Cora. You only have to believe in it. Besides, you have much more than a voice. Your incredible spirit shines from you all the time. It makes you the wonderful mermaid you are. It sounds cheesy, but I look up to you."

Tears slipped down my cheeks, but they were tears of happiness. I changed out of the top and held it out to Rachel. "Take it with you," she said.

"On no," I told her. "I can't keep it at my cave. I'm afraid with all the chaos and my sisters around, it might accidentally get wrecked. I need all the help and magic I can get!"

She laughed, but took it back and hung it in her dad's closet. "I'll bring it to school tomorrow so you can wear it for your dress rehearsal."

I hugged her on my way out of her cave. "You are such a good friend," I told her.

"So are you," she said. "See you tomorrow!"

I swam home with an extra flick in my tail and a huge smile on my face. With that extra bit of magic, I had all the confidence in the world!

Chapter Twenty-Seven

The next day at school, I put on the top
before rehearsal. Rachel swam to the door of the
gymnasium and peeked inside to watch the others'
reaction. The other merkids were thrilled. They
immediately surrounded me and raved about the
shimmery, magical top. Even Regina swam over and
nodded her approval, but she swam away quickly.

After the fussing was over, we ran through
the singing number and my voice held the notes
perfectly. The top really was magical!

When the rehearsal finished, I changed into my regular top. Then I told Shyanna I had to take the special one straight to Rachel. Shy said she'd come with me.

Rachel's dad greeted us at the door and smiled when I gushed about the magical top. "You would make my wife proud," he said, smiling. "Rachel's in her room."

I wanted to surprise Rachel, so I lifted my finger to my lips to tell Shy to be quiet. We quietly swam around the corner to her room and spotted Rachel on her bed. She was lying down with her head on her pillow, and she was weeping as if her heart was breaking into two.

Shyanna and I stopped. Rachel must have sensed us because she looked up. She immediately sat up straight, sniffled, and wiped her tears away.

"Hi, guys," she said, trying to sound cheerful. "What are you doing here? I think there's something in my eye."

"What's wrong, Rachel?" Shyanna asked.

We both swam to Rachel's bed and floated gently down beside her.

"What is it?" I asked.

"It's nothing. Nothing. How did they like the shell top?" she asked.

I crossed my arms. "You know they loved it. But we are not going to pretend that nothing is wrong. You're upset. And I think I know why."

Rachel's chin dropped, and she wouldn't look at Shyanna or me.

"It's Regina, isn't it?" I asked. "What did she do?"

"I don't want to ruin your happiness," Rachel said and her bottom lip quivered.

"We're best friends," I said. "If something is making you unhappy, we have to do something about it. After all, I certainly don't want to hear more talk of you going off to live as a human again. That was just crazy talk."

"Spill," Shyanna told her.

Rachel swallowed and looked at me. Then she lowered her eyes.

"Rachel," I said. "Please tell us."

"Regina saw me watching the dress rehearsal," Rachel whispered. "She told me to leave. She told me half humans couldn't represent a mermaid kingdom, and she didn't want me ruining her practice."

My mouth dropped wide open. I glanced at Shyanna, who looked shocked too.

"She actually said that?" I asked.

Rachel nodded. She looked miserable.

"I'm quitting the Spirit Squad," Shyanna said. "If that is how the leader is treating merpeople, I don't want any part of it."

"Me too," I said as my heart twisted. It hurt to think about not competing, but it wasn't worth all of this unhappiness. "Happiness and friendship are what being a mermaid is all about," I told Rachel. "Not meanness or discrimination. Nobody should have to deal with that."

"You can't quit," Rachel insisted. "It's okay. I'm fine. Maybe I took it wrong. I'm just feeling sorry for myself. It doesn't mean you two are going to give up your dream."

Shyanna looked at me. We both knew it was more my dream than hers. But I shook my head.

"No. What Regina said is not okay. It's not okay. I can't believe the others feel this way too."

"Neither can I," Shyanna said.

I jumped up with a new determination. "I can't let this happen. I need to figure things out."

"Cora?" Shy called and swam quickly after me.

"It's okay," I whispered to her. "You stay here with Rachel. She needs one of us. I'm going to have a special meeting with Cassie. If anyone can help with this, she can."

Shy nodded. "Okay," she said. "Good luck."

Chapter Twenty-Eight

I swam straight to Cassie's cave. She answered the door.

"Why didn't Rachel Marlin make the Spirit Squad?" I asked, not wasting any time.

Cassie glanced around the kitchen, looking really uncomfortable. "I guess some of the other merkids didn't think she was good enough for the team?"

I pressed my lips tight and spoke slowly, trying not to be too angry at Cassie. "Are you aware of how talented Rachel is?"

Cassie sat down across from me, wrapping her long blond hair around her finger, and avoided looking at me. "I know. Trust me, I wanted to have her on the team. I was outvoted."

"By Regina?" I asked.

"I don't think I'm supposed to say," she said.

"Well," I said angrily, "tell me this. Is it because Rachel's mom was human?"

Cassie's cheeks turned bright red. "I don't know, Cora. She didn't come right out and say that."

"What other reason could there be? She's got a great voice and great attitude. Plus, she's a great mermaid," I said.

Cassie sighed and shrugged. "I think maybe you should talk to Regina," she said. "There's not much I can do." She blinked at me with wide eyes, and I saw the sympathy in them. As if she wanted to help.

"Could you arrange a meeting for the whole Spirit Squad right away?" I asked. I wasn't going to let it go. I couldn't ignore it.

Cassie swam up. "Regina isn't going to be happy, but I'll see what I can do," she said.

* * *

Within an hour, Cassie had managed to get everyone over to her house.

"I've called a special meeting," I said to everyone gathered in Cassie's kitchen.

Regina swam to my side. "I'm not sure why you're calling a special meeting when you're clearly not the team leader," she said.

Cassie swam to my other side. "Let her speak, Regina." She glanced out to the Spirit Squad. "Raise your hand if you want to hear what Cora has to say."

Shyanna's hand shot up first. Slowly, other hands went up in the air. It wasn't everyone, but it was enough for me to continue.

"I don't think I need to remind you that we are a team," I said. "The qualities we are trying to display are pride and joy for the Mermaid Kingdom."

The merkids around the kitchen nodded and a couple even whistled their approval.

"We're competing against the best singers and dancers and performers in the entire Mermaid Kingdom," I went on. "And we should have the most spirited merpeople representing us."

"We all know that, Cora," Regina said, rolling her eyes. "That's why we picked everyone here. And that's why I've been nagging you about your performance. We want to win."

"Exactly," I said. "And if we really want to win, we need Rachel Marlin on our team. She has one of the best voices in the entire kingdom, and she lives here in Neptunia. I'd like to know why she wasn't selected to be on our team in the first place."

The room was totally silent for a moment.

"Her voice isn't the problem," one of the mergirls blurted out. Everyone looked at her, and her cheeks went as red as lobster tails. She glanced at Regina with fear in her eyes.

"What exactly is the problem, then?" I asked, staring directly at Regina.

"Oh, come on." Regina rolled her eyes again. "She's — well, she's different."

"We're all different," Shyanna said. She swam to the front and floated close to me.

"Rachel is half-human," Regina said. "No one else is different like that."

"So Rachel really was excluded from the Spirit Squad because she's half-human?" Shyanna asked.

No one was brave enough to say anything or stand up to Regina.

"Why would that even matter?" I asked.

I didn't want to believe Rachel had been right. But no one was denying it.

I looked around the room. "I'm so ashamed," I told them. "This is no way to treat anyone."

"Well, if that's the way you feel . . ." Regina held out her hand and studied the glitter on her nails.

"You bet that's the way I feel," I said.

"Me too," Shy said. "Come on, Cora. Let's go."

We swam out of there together.

"I can't believe everyone in our school feels this way. It's just not right," Shyanna said sadly as we swam away.

"I don't believe everyone does. We have to go to the Queen," I told her. "We have to talk to her. This isn't right."

Chapter Twenty-Nine

Even though we showed up at the castle unannounced, the Queen agreed to see us right away when we told her guard it was about the Neptunia Spirit Squad.

We told her the whole story. "And that's why we decided to come to you," Shy finished.

"Oh dear," said the Queen. "Rachel is such a lovely mergirl. And a beautiful singer too. You three did such a great job at my concert and at the talent show. I wondered why she wasn't selected to represent our castle. Her father must be upset."

"I don't think he knows yet," I told the Queen.

She tapped her finger on her chin, thinking.

"Well," she finally said. "I can't force the team to add Rachel." She smiled. "But there may be another solution." She paused for effect. "You could form a new group."

Shyanna and I looked at each other. "A new group?" I repeated.

The Queen nodded. "Each castle is allowed to enter more than one team. We never have before because we're one of the smaller castles. But . . ." She tilted her head slightly. "It can be done."

Shyanna and I smiled at each other. That just might work!

"We could recruit all the merkids in Neptunia who wanted to be on the Spirit Squad, but who didn't make it or were afraid to try out because of Regina," Shyanna said.

I nodded my agreement. "We could do it!"

"It sounds like a good idea," the Queen said. "A Spirit Squad that won't exclude anyone."

She lifted a finger in the air. "I hereby appoint Cora Bass as the team leader for Spirit Squad 2."

"This is amazing!" I yelled.

The Queen smiled and sat up straighter in her chair. "Okay, off with you two." She spoke in her more regal voice and lifted her chin. "You have work to do. And it's time for my diving lessons."

We swam up, thanking her for her time and her great idea. She waved her hand in the air and another mermaid appeared. We both immediately recognized her. The swimming instructor was the Sea Olympic Champion, Sydney Lincoln!

"Oh, and girls?" the Queen called as we swam down the Royal Hallway.

We both turned back.

"Make us proud!"

Shyanna and I swam away and didn't say another word until we were outside the castle. We both stopped at the same time, let out big breaths, and started to giggle uncontrollably.

Just as quickly as I started laughing, I stopped. "Oh my goodness." I put my hand on my chest. "What did we just agree to? Can we even do this in such a short time?"

"I don't know," Shyanna said. "But we have to go tell Rachel the news."

We swam as fast as we could back toward Rachel's cave. "We have some quick recruiting and lots of practicing to do," I added as we raced to her neighborhood. "And I have to call my mom and see if she'll even give me permission to do this."

"You know she will," Shyanna said.

"I don't know," I replied, suddenly worried. "My sisters are a handful, and she needs my help a lot."

"When she hears the whole story, she'll understand how important it is," Shyanna said.

* * *

When we got to Rachel's house, Mr. Marlin answered the door. Shyanna spilled the news, including an exact playback of our conversation with the Queen.

"She's a great Queen," he said, and then the grin on his face stretched wide. "And Rachel deserves to be on a Spirit Squad!"

"Rachel!" we all yelled. "We have work to do!"

Rachel was thrilled about the new group. Her dad even offered to help coach us once we got more people together. Shy and I called our mothers, and as Shy predicted, my mom was more than happy to give me the night off from babysitting for emergency recruitment for the new Spirit Squad. She said she'd manage without me as long as I needed to make my new group work. I heard the pride in her voice, and my heart swelled.

Shyanna's mom was happy too, and promised to make our entire group matching seashell headbands.

"By the way," Rachel told me, "that top you borrowed isn't magic. The magic comes from believing in yourself. Your singing was all you."

"No way!" I said. "You are pretty sneaky, Rachel."

"Magic or not, we have lots of work to do," Shyanna said. "Let's get started!"

We sat down and came up with a list of everyone who had tried out for the Spirit Squad but hadn't made it. We added a few names of merkids who we knew would love to be on the team, but were afraid of Regina.

Once we had our list, we swam through the entire castle, going door to door to personally ask the mermaids and merboys on our list if they wanted to join our group.

"It's going to be lots of work," we warned each of them. "We'll have to put in extra hours to be ready in time for the swim meet. We only have a few days."

Some kids didn't want to do it. But many did. By the end of the night, we had an enthusiastic and complete team. As team leader, I had to figure out what to do with them in a very short time.

It was up to me. I wondered if I could handle it.

Chapter Thirty

Regina laughed when we told her we were resigning from her team and starting a new Spirit Squad.

"I have the entire gymnasium booked," she said with a toss of her hair. "I can't afford to share it. You'll have to find somewhere else to practice."

"No problem," Rachel told her. "We don't need it."

The team agreed to meet at Walrus Waterpark after school to practice. Our first practice proved we had a team with a lot of heart and oodles of spirit.

Everyone was focused and willing to work hard to learn a routine in a short time. The only trouble was, I couldn't get everyone to agree to sing the song I'd chosen. I knew it was a hard song, but it was one of my favorites.

Instead of wasting time arguing about it, we agreed to work on the dance routine while we thought the song over.

I showed everyone the choreography I'd come up with. Together we adjusted the moves to fit the skills and limitations of our team members. We all worked together, improvising and improving the moves.

The results were astonishing. It was obvious the dance routine was going to be our biggest strength as a team. All the merkids worked together. Our willingness to help each other shine and show off our differences was a definite advantage. We left our first practice with a solid routine that everyone loved.

Shyanna, Rachel, and I left together. As soon as we were out of the park, I burst into tears.

"Cora? What's wrong?" Shyanna asked.

"I'm happy, tired, and a little stressed," I said as I cried like a little baby. "I can't even get everyone to agree on a song, and we only have three days left to learn everything."

Rachel swam in front of me. "Don't be silly, Cora. You put together the most amazing routine I've ever seen. You had everyone taking ownership and working together. You were great."

"I'd like to help," a soft voice said.

I sniffled and looked up. It was Cassie Shore.

"I quit the Neptunia Spirit Squad." She looked at Rachel. "I knew it was wrong — why you didn't make the team. I'm sorry I didn't stick up for you sooner. I think it's awesome that you're half-human."

"It's okay," Rachel said quietly. "And I appreciate you saying that."

Cassie nodded. "I'm on your side."

Rachel smiled. "There shouldn't be any sides. We're all merpeople."

Cassie turned to me. "I saw you practicing, and I couldn't help noticing that you were having trouble with your song. I would love to help."

"That's right! You're a songwriter!" I shouted.

Cassie nodded.

"On one condition," I said. "I think our group will do better if Rachel is our team leader. Can you work with her to rewrite the song and help her teach it to the rest of the group?"

Rachel gasped. "Really, Cora? You want me to be team leader?"

"You're the best singer," I said. I glanced at Shyanna. "Well, you and Shy."

Shy laughed. "It's okay. Rachel is good. And she's much better at performing than I am. It's a great choice, Cora!"

The four of us put our hands out and piled them on top of one another in a perfect team huddle.

"We still have lots of work to do," I said. "But I'm glad we're all doing it together."

Chapter Thirty-One

"Mermen and mermaids, merboys and mergirls, welcome to the Mermaid Kingdom Festival to celebrate our one-hundredth anniversary," yelled the King of Caspian Castle. "First to compete, from Neptunia Castle, Spirit Squad 2!"

The crowd cheered. I glanced at Shyanna. She looked like she was about to be sick. Stage fright was hard for her.

"It's okay, Shy. You're far from alone. And you always do great," I whispered.

She nodded, took a big breath, and swam out into the giant field we would be performing in. From the opposite end of the field, Rachel swam to meet her in the middle. As rehearsed, we were all quiet and still, and then the two of them opened their mouths and started to sing.

The rest of the team swam in fast, doing flips over each other like a giant game of leapfrog. Then Rachel rolled out a big ball of glowing plankton that went off like fireworks. The effects were amazing, and the crowd roared with approval.

The whole team started singing the song that Cassie had composed and Rachel had taught us, and we moved together in a giant wave of motion. We had even added special effects to our routine by using lots of glowing creatures.

There were a few mistakes in our performance here and there, but the crowd was cheering so loudly that I don't think anyone noticed the glitches. I could not believe it was happening.

The finale came quickly, and we all worked together and jumped and sprang off each other like we rehearsed. The final roar of our team could be heard throughout the entire kingdom. "Neptunia!" we shouted as one.

After the crowd settled down, the swim meet got underway. There would be a few more events, and then the other Spirit Squads would perform their routines. I was excited to see what the other groups had put together.

Our team huddled together once we swam off the field. "I'm so proud of every single one of you!" Rachel said. "No matter what happens!"

Merpeople from every castle flocked over to congratulate us. Regina swam by, her nose in the air. "I noticed so many errors in that first performance. How embarrassing," she said to her new co-captain, loud enough for us to hear.

"Yeah, but the performance was pretty spectacular," the co-captain said. "All those special effects and moves were ambitious for a group that just got together. And those mermaids can really sing!"

Rachel giggled. "She won't be co-captain long," she whispered to me.

Our entire team was sitting together when they announced the winner. It was the team from Hercules Castle. Their routine had been the best.

Shyanna swam over to us then. "Rachel! Guess who showed up to surprise you? He was in the crowd and saw our performance."

"Owen's here?" Rachel asked, grinning.

"He didn't know what time we performed so he got here early. He's only got his tail for another hour, so come on." Shy grabbed Rachel's arm. "Come on, Cora!" she shouted to me.

"I'll be there in a minute. I have to find my family!" I called and waved them off.

Everyone around me was gone, and I closed my eyes and took a deep breath to enjoy the moment.

The pace had been crazy over the last few days, but it had been worth it. Our performance was over, and we'd done really well.

When I opened my eyes, my mom was swimming toward me. She was alone, which truly never happened. "Where are the girls?" I asked.

She smiled. "Your sisters are with your father. He needs some practice handling all of them at once. He took some time off of work so I could come and see you." She winked and floated to my side. "That was an amazing show!"

I put my head on her shoulder, enjoying having her all to myself. "Thanks, Mom. I wanted to make you proud. We didn't win, but that's okay. We have lots of heart, but other teams had more time to train. There are a lot of other competitions left."

Mom put a finger under my chin and looked right in my eyes. "You stuck up for your friend. You made difficult choices, and you did the right thing. Like you always do. You make me prouder than you can even imagine!" She softly hummed the song we'd sung. "You're the best daughter and the best big sister a family could have."

"Thanks, Mom," I said, giving her the biggest hug I could.

"I love you, Cora," she said.

As we swam away, I couldn't stop smiling.

Legend of Mermaids

These creatures of the sea have many secrets. Although people have believed in mermaids for centuries, nobody has ever proven their existence. People all over the world are attracted to the mysterious mermaids.

The earliest mermaid story dates back to around 1000 BC in an Assyrian legend. A goddess loved a human man but killed him accidentally. She fled to the water in shame. She tried to change into a fish, but the water would not let her hide her true nature. She lived the rest of her days as half-woman, half-fish.

Later, the ancient Greeks whispered tales of fishy women called sirens. These beautiful but deadly beings lured sailors to their graves. Many sailors feared or respected mermaids because of their association with doom.

Note: This text was taken from The Girl's Guide to Mermaids: Everything Alluring about These Mythical Beauties *by Sheri A. Johnson (Capstone Press, 2012). For more mermaid facts, be sure to check this book out!*

About the Author

Janet Gurtler has written numerous well-received YA books. *Secrets Under the Sea* is her debut book for the middle-grade reader. She lives in Calgary, Alberta, near the Canadian Rockies, with her husband, son, and a chubby Chihuahua named Bruce. Gurtler does not live in an Igloo or play hockey, but she does love maple syrup and does say "eh" a lot.

About the Illustrator

Katie Wood fell in love with drawing when she was very small. Since graduating from Loughborough University School of Art and Design in 2004, she has been living her dream working as a freelance illustrator. From her studio in Leicester, England, she creates bright and lively illustrations for books and magazines all over the world.